THE
EVIL
IN
YOU

THE
EVIL
IN
YOU

JUTTA MARIA HERRMANN

Translated by Jozef van der Voort

 **THOMAS & MERCER**

Text copyright @ 2019, 2020 by Jutta Maria Herrmann
Translation copyright © 2021 by Jozef van der Voort

Previously published as *Böse Bist Du* by Edition M in Germany in 2020. Translated from German by Jozef van der Voort. First published in English by Amazon Crossing in 2021.

Published by Thomas & Mercer, in collaboration with Amazon Crossing, Seattle

www.apub.com

Amazon, the Amazon logo, Thomas & Mercer and Amazon Crossing are trademarks of Amazon.com, Inc., or its affiliates.

ISBN-13: 9781542029759
ISBN-10: 1542029759

Cover design by The Brewster Project

Printed in the United States of America

First edition

THE
EVIL
IN
YOU

Prologue

At long last, the two of them back away from her. Are they just pausing for breath before they start tormenting her again? No, thank God, they're turning away. They walk off and she quickly loses sight of them between the tree trunks.

She's on her own.

Stop! Wait! You can't leave me like this!

She tries to scream, but the words die away in her throat and she can barely manage a squeak. Terror wells up inside her, her heart thundering like a cannon.

She pulls frantically at the ropes. The coarse fibres cut deep into her wrists. Blood trickles down her hands, drips on to the forest floor.

Soaked in spit, the gag in her mouth expands, pressing into her throat. She retches; she's on the verge of choking.

Greedily, she sucks in air through her nostrils, though she's whimpering in pain with every breath. That last blow to her face must have broken her nose.

A sudden noise makes her freeze. She lifts her head to listen. There's rustling – a little distance away, but getting closer. Are they coming back?

Hope flares up inside her – but also fear. Paralysing fear. What are they going to do to her? Murder her in cold blood? Just like her friends? Her eyes flicker from side to side in panic. The shadows between the trees seem to creep towards her. There's movement in the undergrowth to her left. She hears voices, familiar laughter. But that's impossible. They're all dead.

The rustling gets louder, seems to be coming from everywhere at once. Something cold lands on her head. A plop of water. It's raining.

More and more drops start to land on her, pattering against the leaves on the ground. The wind moans, lifting the branches of the trees and shaking the water from their foliage.

Within seconds, she's soaked to the skin. Her tears mingle with the rain running down her face.

She tugs again at the ropes and feels the bark of the tree digging into her back, tearing holes in her T-shirt.

She's tired. Exhausted. *If only I could sleep*, she thinks. But the pain is like a raging beast inside her.

Please come back. Do whatever you want, but don't leave me here on my own.

Her eyelids flicker and droop and she slips away, sliding ever deeper into the comforting darkness.

The rain has stopped by the time she opens her eyes again. Mist hugs the ground, and mosquitoes dance in front of her in the early rays of the rising sun. Thousands of them. They buzz around her head, settling on her face, crawling into her ears and nose, feasting on her exposed arms and legs. She starts to whimper again. The itching is enough to drive her out of her mind.

Please. Come back. I can't take this anymore.

How long has she been here? A day? Two days? Hardly any time at all, and yet it feels like a lifetime.

Her eyes close again. This time when she opens them, it's already dark. An ocean of stars is glittering overhead.

There's no more pain now; she feels strangely disconnected from her body. Even the wild boar emerging from the woods ignore her as they root through the soil at her feet.

15 YEARS LATER

1

Ever since I was little, I've loved Christmas markets more than anything else in the world. My mum would always hold on tight to my hand to stop me getting lost in the crowds. Breathing in the smell of candied almonds, cinnamon and grilled bratwurst, we would stop at every stall and examine the goods on display. I would stare hungrily at all the delicious treats, run my fingers over the textured beeswax candles with their honeycomb patterns and marvel at the beautiful Christmas tree ornaments. Everything shimmered and sparkled, as far as the eye could see. Even people's faces seemed to glow under the coloured lights.

And it had to be cold, of course. Exactly like today. It's just started snowing, in fact. Thick flakes whirl drunkenly from the sky only to melt the moment they touch the ground. It's the first time I've been out in such a large crowd in a long while. My stomach is fluttering with anxiety, but it's not so bad actually. I'm just one person among many. No one's taking any notice of me. No one wants to do me any harm. With these thoughts playing on a loop in my head, I wander across the square and am amazed at how easy it feels.

I stop in front of the swing ride and watch as a woman my age lifts a little girl into one of the seats and pulls the chain across to keep her safe. The child claps her hands with glee and the woman strokes her tenderly on the cheek before stepping back. A whistle blows and the ride gathers speed, all the children beaming and whooping with joy. It gladdens my heart to see it, it truly does.

My eyes fall on a small boy and girl standing hand in hand to one side of the crowd of waiting parents. Their wistful expressions as they watch the chairs whirling round and round over their heads call up memories of my own childhood. We weren't poor exactly, but Mum really had to count the pennies when I was little, so we could only ever afford a bag of candied almonds and a ride on the carousel. On a whim, I go up to the two children.

'Are you here on your own?'

They gaze up at me and shake their heads, their little faces ruddy-cheeked from the cold. The girl points with one pink mitten off to her right, where I see a couple standing by the shooting gallery. The man's just picking up the gun and taking aim.

'Daddy's trying to win a rose for Mummy,' says the boy, rubbing his red nose.

'Have you had a go on the swing ride?' I ask.

'No,' the girl squeaks.

'Daddy says we can't afford it,' the boy adds mournfully.

But he can waste his money on target practice. I shoot an angry glare at the laughing couple.

'Wait here.'

I buy two tickets from the counter, then come back and press them into the kids' hands.

'These are for you,' I say.

'Does that mean we get a go?' The boy peers sceptically at the piece of paper.

'Thank you,' his sister cuts in, her face breaking into a huge smile. 'Thank you so much.'

'Off you go then!' I reply with a smile. I don't need to say it twice. With one last 'Thank you', they dash off towards the ride.

They've got good manners, at any rate. One small point in the parents' favour.

It's touching to see the boy help his sister into a chair and then carefully fasten the safety chain over her lap. After that, he hops into his own seat beside her. Slowly the ride starts to inch round. The two children wave to me, their faces bright with pleasure. I wave back and walk on, a warm glow in my belly. My anxiety has melted away.

On the spur of the moment, I decide to treat myself to a mulled wine. A little reward for being brave enough to follow my therapist's advice and venture out here on my own. Feeling positively cheery by now, I join the queue in front of the stand. At the shooting gallery over the way, the children's father gallantly presents his wife with a tacky plastic rose. They don't seem to have registered that their kids are no longer waiting by the ride.

A sudden piercing scream makes me start and I whirl around. A young girl is running towards me, hair streaming, eyes filled with panic. She looks so like . . .

For a fraction of a second, my heart stops. Something in my head goes *click*. In my mind's eye, the lake drifts into view, the water dyed blood-red by the setting sun. An icy shiver runs through me.

And then I see him.

Bursting out from between two stalls, he moves towards me with jerky, staccato steps, his breath floating like a veil of white over his mouth. In spite of the cold, he's wearing a white short-sleeved shirt, along with his usual grey chinos. On his face, there's the same unctuous smile, cruel and kindly all at once. The sight of him leaves me paralysed with shock. Just like every time.

Leander.

He stops, folds his arms and stares at me with his bright, gleaming eyes. Smiles his malevolent smile.

I know he's not real. He can't be. He's a relic from my past. A projection of my fear. Every time it happens, I repeat these words in my mind like a silent mantra. Always the same words. Only I can't seem to find them today.

Run! a voice roars at the back of my mind. But my legs won't listen. I stand there like a statue, transfixed by Leander's gaze.

Time seems to stand still.

There's a loud bang. A shot. The invisible cord between us snaps and at last I come to. I spin on my heels, shove someone blindly out of the way and run for it.

When I come back to my senses, I'm in a side street, gasping for breath, bracing myself against a lamp post.

Someone grabs my arm to stop me from falling. I hear a voice, muffled and distant somehow.

'Are you all right? Should I call an ambulance?'

I manage to shake my head and cough out the words, 'No, no, it's OK.' And then I vomit all over the shoes of this poor Good Samaritan.

2003

We'd been cycling along the narrow, bumpy, dusty path through the woods for what felt like an age. More than once, I'd nearly been jolted off my bike by the thick tree roots that coiled like snakes across the sun-baked ground. My sweat-soaked top was clinging to my back under my heavy rucksack and my tongue felt like a small furry animal. The heat that had settled on Berlin over the last few weeks, and which we were doing our best to escape, seemed to have penetrated every inch of the forests of Brandenburg. No chirping crickets, not one twittering bird. There wasn't a breath of wind. Only a handful of bees buzzed from flower to flower along the path. Now and then, we'd hear a rustle from the edge of the woods, like that of a bird hopping through the dry undergrowth.

This whole expedition was Paul's stupid idea. My friends had decided against booking a plane to some far-flung location out of respect for my limited means, but deep down I felt more shame than gratitude at their forbearance. I was sure they meant well, but it only seemed to lay even more stress on my status as an outsider, what with my working-class parents and all that. And not for the first time either.

Whatever . . .

Our little clique would be disbanding soon enough in any case. This would almost certainly be our last trip together before we headed our separate ways for a long time. Maybe even forever. The others were moving to Paris to study at the Sorbonne. Juli's face took on this totally blissed-out expression whenever she started rattling on about the French way of life. It made her look kind of crazy. Paul had originally planned to spend the whole summer in Berlin but had changed his mind at the last minute, much to my disappointment. He never said why, but it figured. Juli had probably kept nagging him until he gave in. The twins couldn't stand to be apart for long and I was never going to get a look-in – that much had been clear from the start. But it still stung, of course.

That meant I'd be staying on in Berlin on my own, working at McDonalds until my own course started, and keeping my fingers crossed that my student loan application – which I'd submitted at the eleventh hour – would still be approved. Though it almost certainly would, given how strapped for cash my family was. Yes, it was clear enough which of the four of us had got the shitty end of the stick in life. Right now, however, I wanted to push such gloomy thoughts to one side. I had a few days off and lots of fun to look forward to.

'Jesus, Paul,' Juli grumbled, 'are we ever going to get to this stupid lake of yours? I'm running out of steam here. It's boiling hot and my arse is aching.'

Paul was cycling at the head of our column, with Juli close behind. After her came Erik – Juli's summer shag, as she disparagingly referred to him – followed at some distance by little old me. A few yards back, I could hear Corky, the twins' elderly Labrador, panting away. In a way, it was symbolic of the whole pecking order in our group. Not for the first time, the realisation left a sour taste in my mouth.

Paul held up a hand and cried out, '*Patience, Mademoiselle! Nous y sommes presque.*'

Juli laughed and said something in French that I only half caught, because just then Corky started to growl. I braked, hopped off my bike and turned to see what was up. The dog had stopped dead in the middle of the path, teeth bared. Before I could call him to heel, he took off into the undergrowth with a surprising turn of speed, his tongue flapping as he ran.

2

What was that? I'm wide awake suddenly – ears cocked, heart pounding, my damp nightshirt clinging uncomfortably to my skin.

Maike darling, where are you?

The voice floats through the room, soft as silk, as if coaxing a cat. Its insistent, cloying tone worms its way into my ears, burrowing deep into my consciousness.

Maike darling, where are you?

He's here. Fear settles over me like a lead weight, squeezing the air from my lungs. My eyes wander through the semi-darkness. Everywhere I look, I see shadows and blurred outlines. Where's he hiding?

It's only a dream – a dream! my brain screams at me. *There's no one here. It's only a dream.*

The tinny buzz of my alarm clock comes as both shock and salvation, and the evil spirits slip away to the dark corners of the room – only to linger there, ready to creep back out another night and tear me to shreds.

I'm left on my own: a trembling, miserable wreck. I haven't even the strength to lift my hand and silence the increasingly shrill sound of the alarm clock. Getting out of bed seems unimaginable. Only when I start to shiver in my sopping nightshirt do I heave my weary carcass from the mattress and drag myself into the bathroom.

I strip off, get into the shower and let the hot water cascade over me. My insides feel like a block of ice. Try as I might, I can't seem to get warm. I brace myself against the tiles with both hands and watch the water trickle over my body, gather in the tray and gurgle down the drain. On mornings like this, I wish I could simply dissolve and spiral down the plughole into the void myself.

When the water starts to run cold, I shut off the tap and step out of the shower. Wrapping myself in my dressing gown, I pad barefoot down the hall. The fluffy terry cloth envelops my skin in its warm embrace.

The living-room door is open, and I feel her presence before I see her. She's squatting on the chair with the wicker seat, her face turned away and her arms wrapped around her legs, quietly humming a tune to herself: 'Tears In Heaven' by Eric Clapton. It's always the same song. Never any other. She looks so fragile and lost, as if everyone's forgotten about her. The sight of her breaks my heart and at the same time makes me angry. I know all too well what she's trying to do. She's trying to make me feel guilty. But it wasn't my fault. It was an accident. I couldn't help it. Why can't she forgive me?

My eyes grow moist. I feel an overpowering urge to walk over to her – to touch her – and I take a step closer and whisper her name. But she's punishing me, ignoring me, singing on in her brittle voice as if I weren't there.

I turn round and leave the room, taking her wretchedness with me, which I will wear like a second skin until we next meet.

In the kitchen, I switch on the coffee machine. While waiting for it to rumble its way up to operating temperature, I walk over to the window and wipe away the condensation with my hand. A flower of frost has bloomed in the corner. Its delicate beauty moves me almost to tears.

Winter has returned overnight. Under the glow of the street-light, the wind whips the snowflakes into a wild dance. The roofs of the houses on the other side of the canal look like they're dusted with icing sugar, while at their feet, huddled close together as if for warmth, two ducks bob on the slate-grey surface of the water.

I drink my coffee by the window, watching my surroundings transform into a dazzling fairy-tale landscape, and like a little girl I dream of a perfect world in which I don't need to be afraid of anything or anyone.

Soon afterwards, on the way to the S-Bahn station, I realise the tune to 'Tears In Heaven' is going round and round in my head. Sometimes I'm able to get rid of it pretty quickly, but I can't seem to manage it today. No doubt it'll follow me throughout the day, bringing up all the memories I want so badly to forget.

The snow is still falling, a thick curtain of it now. I pull my hood down over my face and tuck both hands in the pockets of my coat. The pavements haven't been cleared yet and it's slippery underfoot. I slow down and savour the chill as it finally drives away the phantoms of the previous night. Once I reach the shelter of the covered Oberbaum bridge, however, I pick up my pace. I've been dawdling again and I'm running late. Over my head, a train clatters past. The noise has barely died away when I hear someone calling my name.

I hesitate for a second, but then hurry onwards. Surely I must have misheard. I haven't lived in Kreuzberg for long and I don't know a soul in the neighbourhood. Then I hear it again. Louder now. A woman's voice. This time I stop and turn round. A heavily pregnant woman is moving towards me with an oddly cumbersome gait, her legs spread wide apart. I can see the outline of her belly under her scarlet woollen coat. She's grinning from ear to ear. I frown. I don't recognise her; she must have mistaken me for some-one else. It happens fairly often – I'm kind of nondescript-looking.

Low recall value, as they say in marketing. The stranger catches up with me. She's wearing a white woolly hat over her long brown hair, which curls down either side of her doll-like face with its huge eyes and bold dash of red lipstick. She's also wearing way too much perfume – its scent is so cloying, I can practically taste it.

'You must have the wrong person,' I say.

'I recognised you straight away when you looked over your shoulder by the lights just now. Hello, Michaela,' she says.

The intense blue of her eyes finally jogs my memory.

'Antonia? Toni?'

She nods, visibly pleased that I remember her name.

'It's been years, hasn't it! How are you? Do you live around here?'

'Not bad,' I say, followed by, 'Yes.' That's all I can come up with. Small talk never has been my forte.

We stand there and smile at each other – hers is cheerful, mine probably somewhat pinched. It's always awkward running into people who knew me back then. I worry they're going to ask me about what happened.

Toni definitely knows the story. We were at school together. If I remember rightly, we were in two – no, wait – three classes together: maths, French and biology. Beyond that, we didn't have much to do with each other. Toni was a dazzling star with an enormous circle of friends wheeling round in her orbit, while I was quiet, fairly shy and kept myself to myself. People were quite happy to ignore me even then. Did I envy her? Absolutely.

'Are you heading to Warschauer Strasse too?'

I nod.

She steps forwards and grabs my arm as if we're the best of friends, and I flinch. If there's one thing I hate, it's people invading my space. But she reminds me of a child somehow, with her pink nose and shining eyes, so I relent and slow down to match her waddling gait, though it costs me some effort.

By the time we reach the platform some ten minutes later, I'm up to speed with pretty much everything that's happened in my former classmate's life since we left school. She spent fifteen years in Freiburg, where she went to university and also met and married her oh-so-wonderful David, and the two of them moved back to Berlin a few months ago so he could take up a lucrative job offer.

Toni pauses for breath before resuming her monologue. 'The flat on Skalitzer Strasse is only temporary, of course. David wants our child to grow up in the countryside.'

She pats the curve of her belly fondly and gives me a sweet smile. I nod sympathetically and silently pray for the train to arrive. My head is whirring with the sheer volume of information she's bombarded me with and her incessant chatter is really starting to get on my nerves.

'But that's enough about me,' she says, as if she can read my thoughts. 'Tell me all about you then. How have you been getting on all these years?' She lifts her shoulders and shivers. 'I've thought about you a lot, you know, after what happened, and . . .'

She leaves the sentence hanging in the air and glances over at me. The smile has gone from her lips, giving way to a sheepish expression. Even so, her eyes can't help betraying a glint of fascination. Something inside me clenches. She has zero interest in me, only in my sensational past.

The rumble of an approaching train saves me from having to reply and thankfully Toni doesn't probe any further. On the train, we swap numbers. She gives me her landline.

'I've just traded in my old phone,' she says with a brisk shrug. 'It'll be a few days before the new one arrives.'

I promise I'll call her, but even as I say the words, I curse myself for feeling obliged to go through the motions, for whatever reason. Aside from having been at school together, we have absolutely nothing in common. She seems nice enough, but I don't think we'll ever really be friends.

'Are you still in touch with anyone else from back then?' she asks, before we get to her stop at Alexanderplatz.

I shake my head wordlessly. When I was discharged from hospital after the accident, there was no way I could face going back to my old school. The mere thought of the curious and pitying looks everyone would give me kept me awake at night. And besides, I didn't need to finish my *Abitur* exams to get an apprenticeship as a bookseller, which is what I decided to do instead of going to university.

Toni nods sagely, her eyes moist with compassion. She gives me a breathy kiss on the cheek and clambers awkwardly to her feet. 'Well, see you soon then. I'm looking forward to it already.'

'Yeah, me too,' I reply mechanically.

She waves to me again from the platform, her default smile back on her face. I wave back, feeling like a total hypocrite.

3

'Got any thrillers?'

The customer's hair is scraped back in a dead-straight ponytail and she's gazing up at me expectantly. At a guess, I'd say she can't be any more than sixteen.

'Ye-es,' I reply.

'The gorier the better,' she adds eagerly. 'Anything you can recommend?'

It's not my job to suggest books, only to sell them. I don't say that out loud though, I just think it. Anyone who's experienced that level of violence in real life, like I have, will probably never fathom why people have such a thing for bloodthirsty fantasies.

'Come with me.' I lead the girl over to our crime-and-thriller section and pull a handful of titles from the shelf. 'I'm sure one of these'll take your fancy,' I say. 'Feel free to leaf through.'

'Thanks,' she says, and carries her stack of books over to the sofa in the back of the shop.

My mother is just showing out Frau Wiener, one of our few regular customers. She holds the door open for her as she says goodbye. A few stray books are out on the counter and I start putting them back on the shelves.

'So what's putting you off meeting up with her?' Mum asks from behind my back.

I heave an inward sigh. What on earth made me tell her I'd bumped into Toni? I should have known she'd only start harping on again. She's already getting into her stride.

'It's time you got back out there, my love. You've shut yourself off from the world for far too long. It isn't good for you. People need company, conversation, encouragement. We're not designed to spend our lives on our own. Loneliness doesn't just make you eccentric, it makes you ill too.'

I let her burble on, barely listening to what she's saying. It's always the same, every time.

She means well, of course, and in a way she's right: I have turned into something of a hermit over the last few years. If it weren't for Mum, Robert and the bookshop, I'd never see anyone at all. But Toni, of all people. What would we possibly have to talk about? I don't have kids or a partner. I just can't see us making any kind of connection.

With my finger, I nudge a book back in line with its neighbours. The thriller fan is totally absorbed in one of the novels I gave her. She's staring at the page like she's hypnotised.

My mother brings a stack of paperbacks over to the till. Only then do I notice how pale she is. Her eyes are red as if she's been crying, and there are dark, bluish bags underneath them. Deep furrows are etched into her face.

'Is everything OK, Mum? You look tired.'

She rubs her hands over her face and makes a noise that sounds like a sniff. 'I'm more than tired. Robert and I were up half the night talking.'

'Fighting tooth and nail again, you mean.'

She gives me a weak half-smile and shrugs resignedly. 'Don't exaggerate now.'

I raise my eyebrows.

'OK, fine, we were fighting,' she admits, 'but we've already patched things up.'

Robert is my mother's partner. He's pathologically jealous and makes her life a living hell with his ridiculous paranoia. I have no idea what she sees in him. Sometimes I wonder if he's got some mysterious hold over her, like a dark secret only he knows about – something that keeps her chained to his side. Though that seems unlikely to me. My mum is not one of those people with something to hide. She probably just stays with him because he owns the building where the bookshop is. Robert lets her rent the premises for next to nothing, or else we'd have had to shut up shop a long time ago. And that would absolutely break my mother's heart.

'You should just end things with him. Or are you worried he'll raise the rent?'

'No, no, that's not it,' she replies quickly.

Too quickly, I think.

She avoids catching my eye and tucks a stray wisp of hair behind her ear. 'You don't understand. Robert's been a rock to me for all these years. You don't just throw something like that away. And he truly loves me, even if you'd rather not believe it.'

'So why have you never moved in together?'

The bell jingles above the door of the shop as I ask my question and Mum turns away to greet the customer.

Like all empathetic people, my mother has a strong need to get on with everybody. She tries to see the good in people and she mostly manages it too. Sadly I haven't inherited her philanthropic genes. I expect I take after my father in that respect, though I never got to know him. All I know is that he suffered from depression and killed himself shortly before I was born. Mum doesn't like to talk about him. At one point, I even suspected he wasn't dead at all, but had run away instead.

When I was little, I often used to imagine that he would turn up one day and whisk me away with him. I dreamed he'd have all the things that my mum couldn't give me. Money, and lots of it – enough to make my every wish come true. He'd have an amazing house with a huge garden and he'd buy me a dog too – something I so desperately used to want, but which Mum always refused to get me.

Then one day, when I was twelve or thirteen, I came across a battered old suitcase in the basement. Inside were a couple of pulp thrillers, two broken lighters, a Swiss army knife and a handful of photos of my parents together. They looked terribly young and so happy. I felt an odd pang when I looked at it.

I nearly didn't spot the compartment in the bottom of the suitcase. That was where I found the obituary notice that had been cut out of the newspaper, though it had gone yellow, and the newsprint had faded so much that all I could make out was the year he died. 1985. The year I was born. My beautiful fantasy shattered into a million pieces in one fell stroke. Beneath the newspaper clipping was an object wrapped in black cloth. It was a pistol. I could hardly bring myself to touch it at first. After a while, I decided to lift it out carefully, only to instantly let it fall again. It felt so strange holding a weapon in my hands. Had my father shot himself with it? I never worked up the courage to ask, but I did take the gun. Though only much later on.

The phone rings, dragging me from my trip down memory lane and back into the bookshop. We've got so much on this morning that I forget all about my meeting with Toni, so I'm all the more surprised when the door opens shortly before my break and she walks into the shop.

'Toni! What are you doing here?' I ask in surprise.

She smiles, peels off her woolly gloves and shoves them in her pockets. 'Oh, I was just in the area and thought I'd pop by.'

'How did you know I work here?' I don't recall mentioning our little store to her earlier on. Has she been spying on me?

'I'm psychic, didn't you know?' she replies with a cheeky grin, before peering around the shop in curiosity.

Just then, Mum appears from the storeroom with another load of books and we both turn to face her.

'Mum, this is Antonia,' I say reluctantly.

My mother puts the books down and sticks out a hand in greeting. 'Nice to meet you, Antonia. Michaela mentioned you two bumping into each other this morning.'

'Yes! Such an amazing coincidence, wasn't it?' Toni replies, looking to me for confirmation.

'Sure,' I say grudgingly, before adding stiffly, 'Small world sometimes, Berlin.'

'I can't stay, I'm afraid,' Toni says, her voice full of regret. 'I just wanted to ask if you fancy coming round to our place tomorrow night? It completely slipped my mind this morning. We've asked a few friends over.' She looks at me hopefully. 'It's a belated house-warming party.'

'Thanks for the invite,' I say. 'It's kind of short notice, so I'll just have to see.'

'Oh, go on,' says Toni. 'There'll be a few people from school there too. I asked Alexander as well, but he can't make it sadly. He was the one who told me where you work, by the way.'

'Alexander?' I ask in surprise.

Toni nods. 'Think about it, OK?' She gives me an awkward hug over the top of her baby bump. 'I'm really starting to look forward to getting rid of this thing, you know,' she sighs, releasing me from her clutches.

'I'll bet you anything it's a boy,' says Mum with a smile in her voice. 'Have you got a name for him?'

'David and I haven't exactly settled on that yet.' Toni shrugs, throwing her hands up in feigned resignation. 'I'm starting to worry we might have to call him Child Number One. But knowing me, I'll probably give in before that and let David have his way.' She laughs. 'Honestly, it'd be so lovely to see you tomorrow.' She insists that I note down the address. 'Around eight? Though you can come later if you'd rather – it's entirely up to you.'

'I'll try,' I mumble, as I hold the door open for her.

'Bye then, Frau Berger,' she calls over to my mother, who's now up the stepladder and shelving the books from the storeroom.

I close the door behind Toni. I'm glad she's gone. The sheer intensity of her good humour is hard to bear – she has to be putting it on.

'What a lovely young woman.' Mum gets down from the ladder, stands in front of me and plants her hands on her hips. 'You're going to that party tomorrow, even if I have to drag you there myself. And no excuses now. It's your day off on Saturday.'

'I'll think about it,' I reply. 'I promise.'

Mum rolls her eyes and walks away, shaking her head. She knows me well enough to realise that it's no good pressuring me. It'd only make me dig my heels in and refuse point-blank to go.

But right now, I have something more pressing to think about than whether to attend Toni's party. How does Alexander know where I work? The last time I saw him was when I was in hospital after the accident. Our paths have never crossed since. I didn't even know he was still in Berlin. My stomach feels queasy all of a sudden and the sensation lingers for the rest of the day.

2003

'Corky! Here, boy!' I shaded my eyes from the glare and caught a glimpse of the dog in the form of a light-brown shadow slipping off into the trees.

'Oh, leave him.' Erik had stopped too. 'He's probably caught the scent of something. He'll be back soon enough.'

I shrugged – it wasn't my dog after all – and jumped back on my bike. Erik pedalled hard to catch up with the others, who'd gone round the corner already. I followed after more slowly. My legs were getting heavy and my arse was pretty sore by this time too. I was starting to regret ever signing up for this little expedition. Especially as Paul had been more and more distant towards me over the last few days, which left me in a constant panic that he was about to dump me.

A few yards on, the path curved round and widened, and the forest cleared to reveal a lake. The rays of the setting sun scattered across the mirror-like surface of the water, making it glitter as if it were covered in diamonds. I braked and skidded to a halt beside Erik, sliding from my saddle.

Paul turned to look at us. 'Well, what do you reckon? Did I hype it up too much?'

'No, it's incredible!' Juli cried, clapping her hands in glee.

She pulled her dress over her head and dropped it carelessly to the ground. Underneath she was naked, aside from a thong that cleaved her bum into two gorgeous round little buns. Her body was smooth and brown, apart from one round black mole in the middle of her left buttock that looked somehow obscene.

'Who's coming with me?'

She wound her long hair up into a knot and dashed off without waiting for an answer, diving headlong into the lake with a shriek. Paul propped his bike against a tree, stripped off and sprinted after his sister.

I was longing to launch myself into the cool water too, but held back, nervous for some reason. My sweaty hands gripped the plastic handles of my bike, and the right pedal was digging painfully into my calf. Erik hesitated too, propped over his handlebars, his brow furrowed. I followed his gaze out to where Juli and Paul were frolicking around like a pair of puppies and splashing each other.

You'll have to get used to this, I very nearly said. *Don't worry though, you'll be history soon enough*. I quickly bit down on my catty remark. Erik had doubtless twigged already that there was precious little room for anyone else between Paul and Juli.

'Nothing comes between us,' Juli had said to me not so long ago. 'We're like conjoined twins – bound to one another for all eternity.' She was deadly serious too.

'I'll make a start on our tents,' Erik muttered. He wheeled his bike a little further on towards a small patch of grass. I propped my own bike beside the others and eased my backpack off my shoulders. Then I slipped out of my blouse and shorts and wandered down to the lakeside in my bikini. All I could see of Juli and Paul were their heads, floating on the surface of the water some distance away as if detached from their bodies. I waded out a few tentative steps into the lake. The water was colder than I'd expected and the ground beneath my feet felt unpleasantly slimy. Slowly I moved

25

forwards, parting the smooth surface of the lake with my hands and watching the tiny ripples drift away.

An ominous feeling of being watched suddenly came over me. I turned round and scanned the shore. Erik seemed to be busy with his tent. Corky still hadn't reappeared. And then I heard a splash at my back. Before I could react, I felt two hands gripping my ankles underwater. I shrieked in fear and tried to shake them off. Then a shove in my back drove me face-first into the lake. Someone jumped on top of me and pushed my head underwater. I flailed wildly with my arms, but my assailant held me with an iron grip. Just as panic started welling up inside me, they finally let me go. Spluttering, I pushed to the surface, gasping for air.

Juli and Paul were beside themselves with laughter.

'Fuckwits!' I roared at them. 'Are you off your heads?' I smacked my hands down on the water as hard as I could and soaked them both. Inwardly I was boiling with rage, but I forced myself to laugh along with their mean game. I didn't want to start a fight and spoil the mood for everyone.

'Alright, alright, you win!' Paul hollered, shielding his face with his arms.

'Could someone give me a hand maybe?' Erik yelled from the shore. He sounded annoyed.

'Your wish is my command, good sir. I'll be with you at once,' Paul called to him good-naturedly, before blowing a kiss first to his sister, and only then to me. I felt a sharp pang in my belly and the smile I gave him cost me unspeakable effort. But he didn't seem to notice. He grinned at me, slicked back his wet hair and waded to shore.

Juli and I followed slowly. We parked ourselves on the small strip of sand at the water's edge and dried ourselves in the sun while the boys argued noisily over tent pegs and guy ropes.

'Is something the matter?' Juli asked abruptly. Her face was tilted towards to the sun, her eyes half-closed.

'What do you mean?' I scooped up a handful of sand and let it trickle slowly through my fingers.

'Just that you're very quiet,' Juli said, turning to look at me. 'Are you mad because Paul decided to come with me after all?'

'Well, it's not like Paris is on another planet or anything,' I replied, shrugging with studied indifference, though I felt like bursting into tears. I leaned forwards so that my long hair hung over my face like a curtain.

'True,' said Juli. 'Besides . . .' She left the word hanging ominously in the air.

'Besides what?' I asked in alarm.

'Oh, never mind,' she answered with a dismissive wave of her hand.

And that was the end of the conversation as far as she was concerned. Tact never had been one of her strong points. That was something she shared with her brother. The thing was, I knew exactly what she was hinting at. Paul was forever trading in his girlfriends and I'd be no exception. I'd probably been on his kill list for a while already. My throat contracted.

'Where's the dog anyway?' Juli leaped to her feet and peered around. Only now did she seem to notice he was missing. 'Corky!' she called, cupping her hands around her mouth. 'Here, Corky!'

I stood up and swept the sand from my backside with my hands. That was when I spotted them. Two boys I didn't recognise, standing in the trees a little way off and staring at us. I nudged Juli with my elbow.

'Look,' I said, nodding in their direction. 'We're being watched.'

4

The closer I get to the apartment block on Skalitzer Strasse, the more hesitant I become. I'm positively dawdling in spite of the biting wind and the cold that started to chill me just a few steps into my journey. I'm sorely tempted to turn and run straight home to my cosy little apartment. But I push my hands into the pockets of my down jacket and force myself to keep going. Mum's right. It's high time I rejoined the land of the living. I need to meet new people, renew old acquaintances, make friends. I need to free myself from the past – draw a firm line under it – or else they might as well bury me right here and now. Somewhere or other, I remember reading a phrase that sums it up nicely: I need to put more life into my days. On the spur of the moment, I decide that's going to be my new motto. Maybe it'll help me finally banish my demons back to where they belong – consigned to oblivion.

But the nagging certainty that it's simply beyond my capabilities creeps into my thoughts, immediately smothering any small flicker of optimism.

I sigh, biting my lip, and trudge onwards. On the railway line overhead, the yellow caterpillar of the U-Bahn rumbles past, its windows brightly lit. The headlights of the passing cars paint patches of light on the gleaming wet asphalt. According to the weather forecast, temperatures are going to drop below freezing tonight and we can expect dangerously icy conditions. I could slip and break my leg. Once again, I'm forced to suppress with all my might the powerful urge to turn back. And anyway, I wish I had someone by my side. A committed partner who I could talk to and laugh with. A man who'd take me as I am and love me for all my fears and flaws. And I definitely won't find him if I stay at home.

Toni lives just a few hundred yards away from the station at Schlesisches Tor. I stop outside her apartment block and cast my eyes over the plain frontage of the building. With a small handful of exceptions, every window is lit up with the cold blue light of a TV screen. Down at street level, the outside wall is covered with graffiti. Someone's spray-painted a turquoise sea and a golden beach under a deep blue sky over the lintel of the front door, while on either side stand tall palm trees, their green fronds stretching high up the walls.

'Evening, Michaela – what a lovely surprise.'

I'm so lost in thought that the voice makes me jump. I can't help but give a squawk of alarm and my cheeks burn with shame. Am I imagining it, or is it really him? Slowly I turn round.

'Oh, I'm sorry.' He grins at me. 'I didn't mean to scare you.'

'Hello, Alexander,' I say.

I feel a slight shock at the sight of him. It's been over fifteen years since we last met, but he's barely changed. He's the spitting image of Erik, with the same bashful, crooked smile that makes his eyes light up and instantly puts you at ease. He has Erik's red hair and endless freckles too. With his slightly too-big nose and full lips, he's not exactly handsome, but he's certainly attractive.

'You didn't scare me,' I say quickly to reassure him, forcing a smile. 'I'm just surprised to see you here. Toni said you couldn't make it.'

If I'd known he was coming, I would absolutely have stayed at home.

'That's what I told her too, but my appointment got cancelled at short notice.'

'I see.' I point at the panel of buzzers. 'Do you know Toni's surname?' I ask as nonchalantly as I can.

'Not a clue,' he replies. 'And of course I stupidly forgot to ask.' He winks at me and I relax a little.

We examine the name labels together. Our heads are so close, they're almost touching, and the tang of his aftershave hits my nostrils. It's not unpleasant exactly, but I step away from him slightly all the same.

'Here we go,' he says, pressing a button. On the sign beside it, I read *A. & D. Wilhelmsen*. 'That must be them.'

Shortly afterwards, we hear a chirpy voice over the intercom saying, 'Come on up!' and the sound of the buzzer letting us in. Alexander leans on the door, which opens with a faint squeak. Then he ushers me through with an exaggerated bow, and on a whim, I dip into a slight curtsey in return, feeling like a right idiot as I do so. What on earth's got into me? To hide my embarrassment, I turn my back on Alexander and press the light switch.

In tacit agreement, we ignore the lift and trudge up the stairs in silence. The stairwell is eerily quiet. The air is stale and smells rank. You'd be forgiven for thinking the building is derelict, if it weren't for the pram parked outside the door to an apartment on the second floor and the sudden wail of a baby.

Toni is waiting for us in her doorway on the third floor, looking as radiant as ever. Her cheeks are flushed, her eyes sparkling. She's clearly one of those women who thrives on being pregnant; she looks in the pink of health. There's music playing softly in the apartment – some kind of jazz.

Toni accepts Alexander's bouquet of flowers with a merry, 'Oh, you shouldn't have!' I could have brought her a book as a gift, I think shamefacedly.

'It's lovely to see you both,' she says.

Our hostess brushes a strand of hair from her flushed face and kisses me and then Alexander on both cheeks, as if we're her best friends. This is all too much for me already. I'll give myself an hour and then get out of here.

The inside of the apartment is pleasantly warm and smells of grilled food and garlic. We hang up our coats on the near-empty rack and follow Toni through into the living room.

A couple I don't know are sitting on the black leather sofa, holding hands. The woman is heavily pregnant, like Toni. I instantly feel completely out of place. Probably most of the other women coming tonight are expecting too. Toni introduces the couple to me as friends from her antenatal group and tells me two names that I forget within seconds.

Leaning against the windowsill is a slightly chubby guy with a receding hairline and a doughy complexion, whom I only notice when Toni says, 'I don't need to introduce you to Hartmut of course – you two know each other from way back when.'

I don't have the foggiest how I'm supposed to know this man. Were we in the same class at school? Dance lessons, was that it?

'Nice to see you again after such a long time,' he says, and gives me his hand.

I shake it and squeeze out a smile. Hartmut's hand is soft and damp, like a sponge, and I surreptitiously wipe my palm on my trousers. I'm pretty sure he doesn't remember me either, or he wouldn't have been quite so breezy. Anyone who knows me from 'way back when' knows my story too. It was in all the papers and on TV. I had my fifteen minutes of fame, though it was a dubious sort of notoriety I would have given anything to forgo.

'David sends his apologies,' Toni says, her smile looking strained. 'He's stuck in the office and will be joining us later.'

I sit down in one of the two armchairs with their bright, flowery covers, and examine the rest of the room. Cool metal and dark reclaimed wood. Soft plush against leather. It's an unusual look, but there's something to it – though the furnishings don't seem especially child-friendly.

'It's very . . . different, your apartment,' says Alexander, as if voicing my thoughts. He takes a seat in the other armchair.

Toni is about to say something in return when the doorbell goes. 'There's wine, bubbly and that sort of thing in the kitchen. Cold beers in the bathtub,' she tells us somewhat breathlessly as she hurries out of the room.

I can sense Alexander's eyes resting on me and feel increasingly uncomfortable. What will I do if he brings up Erik and the others? If he asks why I didn't want any more to do with him?

I'll just get up and leave. Why should I care what he thinks of me?

But Alexander says nothing, and that doesn't exactly help my nerves either. More and more guests filter in, and pretty soon all the seats are taken. Other small huddles of people stand chatting in the corners.

'Short hair really suits you, by the way,' Alexander announces out of the blue.

I look at him. There's a glint of amusement in his eye. Is he making fun of me?

I twist my mouth into something resembling a smile and say, 'Thanks.'

He lifts himself out of his chair. 'I think I'll go get myself a beer. Shall I bring you one too, or do you fancy something else?'

'I'll have a glass of tap water,' I reply, before immediately correcting myself. 'No, wait – get me a beer.'

Generally speaking, I barely ever drink. At most a glass of prosecco to ring in the new year, or to celebrate a birthday. But I'm so tense right now I can feel a headache brewing. Maybe the alcohol will loosen me up a bit.

I watch as Alexander slouches through the room, hands in pockets, and I notice a few women throwing him lustful glances. I wonder if he's got a girlfriend. Probably not, or he'd hardly have come here on his own. Either way, it makes no difference, as we'll never see each other again after tonight.

Alexander is Erik's younger brother. At some point when I was in hospital, he turned up with a bunch of flowers and wanted to talk about what happened by the lake. I'd much rather have sent him packing; I had absolutely no desire to go over it, least of all with him. But I felt sorry for him somehow, in his boundless grief. He seemed to have loved his brother very much. The problem was that there wasn't an awful lot I could tell him. There were gaps in my recall. Retrograde amnesia, the doctors called it. All the same, Alexander kept visiting – almost every day. He wouldn't let it drop and grew ever more insistent, constantly asking if anything had come back to me yet. Once he even accused me of repressing the memories. If I could have, I'd have thrown him out of the room with my own two hands, but I was still too weak and confined to my bed. I felt helpless, completely exposed to Alexander's probing. On top of that, I could barely stand to look at him anymore. Every time I did, I pictured Erik lying in his tent, covered in blood. Eventually I lost it and screamed at him to just leave me alone. I was downright hysterical – couldn't stop yelling. A nurse came rushing into the room, saw immediately what was going on and asked my visitor to leave. After that, Mum made sure he never came back. I've no idea how she managed it, but I didn't much care. The main thing was that the visits stopped. I haven't seen Alexander since then, but I've thought about him a lot.

Shrieking laughter catapults me from the past straight back into the present. Someone pumps up the volume on the speakers and the bass begins to throb. I look round the room. The first smokers are hunched out on the balcony, puffing clouds into the cold air. I don't know who any of these people are.

Alexander appears with two cold beers, dripping with condensation, and hands me one before perching on the arm of my chair. His seat's been occupied by a dark-haired bombshell who looks like Penélope Cruz. We drink in silence.

Toni appears in the kitchen doorway and claps her hands. 'I hereby declare the buffet open!' she cries.

The room empties in the blink of an eye. Only Alexander and I are left behind. I'm suddenly so conscious of his proximity that I start to feel increasingly anxious. I feel like I should be making some casual, off-the-cuff remark, but for the life of me I can't come up with a thing to say. I take a big swig from my bottle. Is Alexander feeling awkward too?

'It's been a long time,' he says, cutting into my thoughts. 'So how are you?'

'Not bad. And you?'

'Much the same.'

The conversation falters a little until a thought occurs to me and I speak without pausing to think.

'How did you know where I work, by the way?'

The question takes him by surprise, I can tell. He scratches his head and gives a shy smile.

'I'm with the police,' he says finally. 'You can find out things like that pretty easily.'

'But why—?'

'Just because,' he says, interrupting me. 'No particular reason.' He shrugs. 'I can't seem to let go of what happened back then. So I wanted to check if you were still in Berlin and find out what you're doing with your life.'

'I see,' I say. But I don't quite buy it. He hesitated just a touch too long before answering.

We end up talking for quite a while. To my surprise, my shyness melts away and the conversation flows more and more easily. That might have something to do with the second beer Alexander brings me, without my even asking. When the living room gets so full we can hardly hear ourselves speak, we move into the kitchen, where we laugh at the ransacked buffet and take our pick of the leftovers. Alexander tells me about his job as a detective and I try to keep up with anecdotes from my life as a bookseller. But we both steer a wide berth around our shared history.

At some point, I'm astonished to realise just how much I'm enjoying being around Alexander. That pushy boy at the hospital, who fired questions at me with scant regard for my physical condition, has grown into the most charming man. Not only is he actually listening to me, but he's showing genuine interest in who I am. And he's funny too. I feel completely at ease in his company and the same seems to go for him. At any rate, he scarcely leaves my side all evening.

The warm surge of happiness that wells up unexpectedly is so unfamiliar it frightens me. I should probably leave. It's already after midnight. I haven't been out this late in ages. And besides, I feel a little tipsy from the alcohol. I'm sure I've chattered on far too much with Alexander and revealed way more about myself than is good for me.

'I think it's probably time I headed home,' I say.

I put down the empty beer bottle and look around for Toni to say goodbye, but can't see her anywhere. I'll call her tomorrow to thank her again for the invite and tell her how much I enjoyed the evening.

'I'll come with you some of the way,' says Alexander, as he follows me into the living room.

'There's no need,' I say quickly. 'I only live up the road.'

'I'm going to Warschauer Strasse,' he says. 'That's in your direction, isn't it?'

Well, well, well. So he even knows where I live. Or did I tell him that after he told me how he'd recently moved into his late parents' house in Frohnau? Maybe, but I can't say for certain. It really is high time I got home, given the state I'm in.

'Right, yes, I'll be heading that way,' I say.

We dig out our coats from the rack and leave. The party's still in full swing; music and laughter follow us down the stairs. We're almost on the ground floor when pitch darkness suddenly descends. I stumble, cry out and grab hold of the banister to steady myself.

A feeling of disorientation washes over me, as if I'm floating in an endless blackness, with no gravity to hold me down. Panic surges through me. Where's Alexander? I can't see him. Why won't he say something? I open my mouth to call to him, but then I hear footsteps. Muffled words and a male voice. The footsteps draw nearer and the muttering grows more insistent, creeping into my ear. A grey shadow emerges from the darkness.

'Maike darling,' the figure whispers in a velvety soft voice, before repeating the words. 'Maike darling—'

The rest of the sentence is swallowed by the rush of blood in my ears. Sweat breaks out from every pore on my body. A wave of nausea passes over me and my vision flickers. The floor beneath my feet starts to roll, then drops out from under me.

I scream.

5

'Are you all right?'

Alexander's question seems to reach me over vast expanses of time and space. I open my eyes and blink in the light. He's standing at the foot of the stairs and staring up at me, his brow furrowed.

'The light went out,' he said. 'And then you screamed.'

'Sorry.' My voice is rather shaky. 'I get panicky in the dark.'

He nods sagely. 'I expect you'll have that fear all your life,' he murmurs. I can hear the note of pity in his voice and a flash of anger shoots through me.

'Thanks,' I reply, more brusquely than I mean to. 'That's just about the last thing I wanted you to say.'

'Sorry.' Alexander hesitates as if he wants to add something, but then turns and walks briskly off down the hall. I follow after him.

It took me years to pluck up the courage to leave the house. And it was only after Robert took me along to his gun club and taught me to shoot that I gradually began to venture out on to the streets at night on my own, my father's revolver tucked inside my bag. I have no idea if I'd actually use it, if it came to it. Probably not, but it makes me feel safe. Though it doesn't protect me from the occasional panic attack, or the hallucinations that come with them. Luckily the attacks have grown more and more infrequent over the last few years, but they haven't quite stopped altogether unfortunately. I shudder when I think back to my recent trip to the Christmas market and my hasty departure from it.

'Was there anyone else in the stairwell besides us just now?' I ask with feigned nonchalance.

I expect him to say no, but he immediately answers, 'Yeah, there was a man. Why?'

'I heard footsteps.' A hot wave of agitation courses through me. 'What did he say?'

Alexander stops and turns to look at me. 'Why do you want to know?' he asks, perplexed.

'His voice sounded familiar somehow,' I say as casually as I can, but I can tell he doesn't quite accept my explanation.

'I think he was holding a phone,' he says. 'He may well have said something, but I wasn't really paying attention. He went up in the lift.' Alexander points at the grey metal door.

'It doesn't matter anyway,' I mumble, putting an end to the conversation. Even if the man did say something, it can't have been what I thought I heard. I shouldn't have asked about it. That was rash of me.

Alexander gives me a searching look, presumably expecting me to say more. But I can't. I'd rather bite my tongue off than admit that I sometimes hear voices. So I push past him quickly and hurry down the last few steps to the entrance.

An icy wind blows in our faces as we step on to the pavement and I can't help but shiver. The parked cars are covered in a thin crust of ice and the ground is slippery underfoot. With head lowered and shoulders hunched, I walk with careful little steps alongside Alexander towards Schlesisches Tor. I throw him a surreptitious glance. His hands are buried in his coat pockets, his eyes fixed on the street ahead. He seems very unapproachable all of a sudden.

'I'll walk you home,' he announces brusquely.

I open my mouth to protest – it's only five minutes' walk from here after all. Despite how cold and late it is, the streets are pretty busy still, thanks to the countless nightclubs that have sprung up all over Kreuzberg like mushrooms over the last few years. There's really no need for me to be afraid. But I decide to accept his offer. It'd be a shame somehow if our nice evening came to such an abrupt end.

We walk back to my place in silence, as if we've already exhausted everything we had to talk about at the party.

'Here we are,' I say in front of my building, and fumble for my key in the inside pocket of my coat.

'Nice spot,' says Alexander, his eyes roaming over the surroundings. 'Right by the canal. And so quiet.'

'Yes,' I say, my breath forming a cloud. 'Especially considering it's party central just a few streets over,' I add in a weak attempt at humour.

'Well then,' he says, rubbing his hands, which are red from the cold.

'Thanks again for walking me home.'

'No problem,' he says. 'Goodnight. Sweet dreams.'

'You too,' I say.

He gives me a nod and turns to go. To my surprise, I realise I'm disappointed. But what was I expecting? That he'd kiss me goodbye and ask me out on a date?

He goes a few steps, then stops and swings round.

'By the way . . . was it your idea to ban me from visiting you back then?'

His question comes as such a surprise that I don't know how to reply. 'Well . . . I mean . . . It was such a long time ago . . .' I shrug helplessly.

'No, forget it.' He waves his question away. 'It doesn't matter now anyway,' he says, and turns again to leave.

I watch him go. Something inside me wants to run after him, to tell him . . . Well, what exactly? That I'm sorry? Right this minute, it'd even be true. I've met a whole new Alexander this evening – a man I feel drawn to in more ways than one. But back then I just felt utterly relieved to be spared any more of his visits.

I unlock the front door and shuffle up the stairs to my flat, suddenly defeated – flat out depressed, in fact – without really knowing why.

I quickly shut the apartment door behind me and lean against it. The narrow hallway is cloaked in darkness. There's still a faint hint of the perfume I put on for the party lingering in the air. Despondency enfolds me, swaddling my chest like a constricting overcoat. A deep sadness takes possession of me, as if someone I dearly love has just bid me farewell for the very last time. My eyes burn with tears.

What's wrong with me? It's not like anything happened. I've had an unexpectedly nice evening – no more, no less. All the same, my encounter with Alexander seems to have knocked me off-balance. It'd definitely be best not to cross paths with him again.

Gradually my eyes adjust to the darkness and the contours of my apartment drift into view. On my right, the coat rack; on my left, the bathroom door; and at the far end, the kitchen.

She's there. I can feel her presence with every fibre of my being. I take off my shoes and coat as quietly as possible and then tiptoe down the corridor. I don't want to see her. Not now. Just outside the door to the kitchen, I hold my breath, crouch down – as if that would make me any less visible – and scurry past.

'You're forgetting me,' I hear her say, her tone full of reproach.

I flinch and close my eyes briefly, feeling a mounting sense of revulsion.

'You can't forget me. I forbid you,' she says mournfully.

I flee into my bedroom and lock the door. Like that'll help. If she wants to get to me, a locked door won't stop her. A chill descends over me and I crawl under the duvet, shivering violently, but I can't seem to get warm. I lie awake, heart pounding, listening out for any small scratch or squeak, any shift in the atmosphere. But all is quiet. The feeling that I'm about to suffocate under the weight of my loneliness grows stronger, and I can't seem to shake it off. At last I drift into a fitful sleep from which I keep waking with a jolt, her plaintive voice still echoing in my mind.

◆　◆　◆

It's well after nine in the morning by the time I wake up, my stomach aching. I feel like a wreck. Maybe I'm coming down with something. Then I could stay in bed for a few days – that's exactly what I need. I drag myself up and shuffle to the bedroom door. Quietly I turn the key and peer out into the hall. No one to be seen or heard. I put my slippers on, pad through to the kitchen and fill the kettle to make camomile tea.

The world outside the window looks every bit as bleak and sombre as I feel inside. A solitary swan is drifting over the ripples that cross the grey water of the Landwehr Canal and slosh against the opposite bank.

Her voice is still echoing through my mind; I can hear her words as clearly as if she were standing next to me.

You're forgetting me.

But she's wrong. I never stop thinking of her. There's hardly a day goes by when I don't see her before me. Strapped to that tree, half-dead. Hardly a day when I don't imagine the agonies she must have suffered before the release of death. These images are so firmly rooted in my brain that they never leave me; I can call them up at any time. I'd give anything to be able to lock them up in some hidden vault of my mind and throw away the key. But I don't think that's possible. These constant flashbacks are a part of me now. I have to live with them – along with the fear that one day they'll drive me insane.

Sitting down at the kitchen table, I fold my hands around the hot mug, sip my tea and try to dispel all these thoughts by remembering the previous night instead. Thinking of Alexander brings a smile to my face. I felt so at ease in his company. It's just a shame the evening came to such an awkward end.

The scene in the stairwell springs unbidden to my mind and I suddenly hear that stranger's voice again. His soft, wheedling tone. An ice-cold shiver runs down my back. Could it have been Leander? I instantly pull myself up. That's pretty far-fetched. What would he be doing in Toni's apartment block, for goodness' sake? Then again, what if he's an acquaintance, or a colleague of Toni's husband? What if he was heading to the party? What if he's a neighbour of theirs even? The thought nags at me. I could ask Toni about it. Tell her about a man I met on the stairs with a gorgeous voice and then describe Leander to her. The description might be enough to remind her of someone.

The clock above the fridge tells me it's just gone ten. Swallowing the last of my tea, I reach for the phone. I wait, listening to the ringing tone, but nobody picks up. Just as I'm about to hang up disappointed, a sleepy male voice at the other end of the line says, 'Hello?'

This must be Toni's husband, David. It occurs to me that I never actually met him last night.

'Oh, I'm sorry – I hope I didn't wake you?' I say bashfully. The party probably went on until the early hours of the morning. 'I was hoping to speak to Toni. Is she there?'

She was clearly waiting next to the phone, because the next thing I hear, barely a second later, is a cheerful, 'Antonia Wilhelmsen.'

'Morning, Toni,' I say.

'Oh, good morning! It's nice to hear from you.'

'I just wanted to thank you for inviting me last night. I had a great time – you made me feel really at home.'

'That's lovely to hear,' she says warmly. 'It's just a pity you left before I got the chance to say goodbye.'

Before I can reply, I hear a male voice in the background.

'Toni darling . . .'

Toni darling?

My blood runs cold. My whole body starts to tremble and I grip the phone as if I'm clinging on to it for dear life.

'Just a second,' Toni says to me. And then, more quietly: 'Yes, honey?'

I hear what sounds like a smack of the lips. He must just have kissed her. I feel sick.

'I'm just going for a run in the park. I'll be back in an hour or so.' His voice rings through to me loud and clear.

It's him.

The handset suddenly feels impossibly heavy. It slips out of my hand and lands on the floor with a dull thud.

2003

The two boys were standing stock-still a short distance away and didn't take their eyes off us.

'What are you staring at?' Juli yelled at them. 'Never seen a naked woman before?' She struck a pose for them, running her hands over her body, defiantly returning their gaze all the while.

'Stop it, Juli,' I hissed.

Paul and Erik joined us and looked across at the two strangers. I hurried over to my bike, pulled my shorts and top over my still-wet bikini and slipped my feet into my sandals.

'Can we help you?' I heard Paul shout. And then, more quietly, 'Come on, Juli, put some damn clothes on.'

I plucked Juli's dress out of the grass, walked back over to the others and pressed it into her hand. Juli rolled her eyes, but put it on without further protest.

The two boys were now sauntering over in our direction. They were a good two or three years younger than us, and kitted out in neatly pressed dark grey chinos with white short-sleeved shirts buttoned up to their necks, making them look like prissy, well-mannered pupils at some nineteenth-century boarding school.

'Hello there,' said the shorter of the two.

'Hi,' Paul and Erik replied, almost in unison.

'My name is Felix.' He gave a slight bow. 'Pleased to meet you.'

Juli giggled next to me. I poked her playfully in the ribs with my elbow and whispered, 'Shh!'

'And this is Leander,' said Felix, gesturing towards his companion.

Leander tucked a strand of hair behind his ear and studiously avoided my eye. His cheeks and forehead were covered in angry-looking acne; he looked like the inside of a pomegranate. I didn't let my glance linger too long.

Paul took it upon himself to introduce the four of us. Then we all stood there in awkward silence.

'Well,' said Paul eventually, 'it was nice meeting you, but this is a private party, if you get my drift.'

'Oh, a party. Are you celebrating something?' Felix enquired politely.

'Yes, we are,' Juli confirmed. 'And you're not invited,' she added, putting stress on every word.

'What a pity.' Felix smiled regretfully. 'We'd have loved to join in the celebrations. Wouldn't we, Leander?'

Felix's companion shuffled his feet and nodded. He hadn't said a word so far. Was he mute? Or just shy?

'The problem is, you see . . .' Felix hesitated and his cheeks went red, as if he was embarrassed. 'Wild camping,' he went on, cocking his thumb towards our tents, 'is banned here. In fact, it's banned throughout the whole of Germany. Isn't it, Leander?'

Once again, Leander nodded, his eyes fixed on the ground in front of his shoes.

'And?' Juli stuck her chin out defiantly. 'Have you seen anyone to stop us?' She gave a grand sweep of her arm at the empty surroundings.

Felix pursed his lips and tilted his head to one side and then the other, as if he were thinking it over. 'OK then, how about a deal?

You give us . . . let's say, a hundred euros, and we'll turn a blind eye on this occasion.'

'In your dreams, mate!' Paul snorted.

'Think about it. Before it gets even more expensive.'

I looked up. This was the first time we'd heard Leander speak. His voice was surprisingly soft.

'OK, guys, time you got going,' said Erik. 'You're starting to get on my nerves.'

The two of them exchanged glances and Felix made a vague gesture towards the forest with his head. Leander nodded, and they wandered off without another word.

I watched them leave with a queasy feeling in the pit of my stomach that we'd got rid of them just that little bit too easily.

The boys were barely out of earshot before Juli started spluttering with indignation. 'What the hell was that all about?' She waggled her index finger over her temple. 'Those two aren't right in the head. A hundred euros – was that for real?'

We goofed around, mimicking Leander's whiny voice, and fell about laughing. The others were all of the mind that it was the last we'd see of the two boys. I had my doubts still, but kept them to myself. I didn't want to be a killjoy, and maybe I was wrong in any case.

While Paul and Erik set about gathering dry wood for the fire we wanted to light on the shore after sunset, Juli and I decided to look for Corky. We were starting to get worried about the old boy. I grabbed the torch from my backpack in case the search took longer than we reckoned.

'Let's go,' I called over to Juli.

She didn't seem to hear me – it was like she was frozen, her eyes fixed on something I couldn't see. Feeling nervous, I walked back to where she was standing.

Felix and Leander had emerged from the woods and were heading towards us. Between them was a dog that Felix was dragging along on a length of coarse rope. It was Corky. He was yapping, tugging at the lead, but Felix yanked him back and he started to whine.

'Shit,' muttered Erik behind us. 'Them again.'

'What do they want?' Paul hissed.

The two boys drew closer. Corky was covered in filth, his fur matted with twigs, and he was limping badly. My eyes fell on the baseball bat swinging in Leander's right hand and a vague anxiety started to creep up inside me. They came to a stop in front of us. Juli crouched down and stroked the whimpering dog on the head.

'What have you done to him?' Her voice was quivering with fury.

'Nothing!' answered Felix, looking down in surprise at the poor little beast beside him. 'What makes you think we've done anything? He's happy as Larry – look at him!'

Juli shot to her feet and slapped Felix full in the face. He let go of the lead and ran his hand over his nose, then stared in bewilderment at the blood on his palm. Corky hobbled over to Juli's side and started to growl, his teeth bared.

'What did you do that for?' asked Felix, staring at Juli in reproach. 'Is that the thanks we get for bringing back your stupid mutt?'

I heard Juli take a sharp breath in, but before she could let rip, Paul stepped in.

'Thanks,' he said. 'It's very kind of you.'

'You're welcome,' said Leander, as Felix tipped his head back, took a handkerchief from his trouser pocket and carefully dabbed his nose.

'You owe us a finder's fee, I reckon,' he said thickly, breathing through his mouth because of the blood. 'How much is a Lab like this worth anyway? A thousand euros?'

'You must be out of your minds,' said Juli. 'Come on, piss off now. I've had enough of this little charade.'

Felix went on undeterred. 'A ten per cent finder's fee is standard. So what with the hundred from earlier, that makes two hundred euros you owe us.'

'Two hundred?' asked Paul sarcastically. 'Is that all?'

'Like my friend just said, the dog is worth so much more to you than that,' Leander declared.

Felix sighed. 'I'm far too generous for my own good.'

I had no idea what game these two were playing with us, but they were starting to properly frighten me. 'Listen, how about we give you fifty euros? That sounds fair to me. What do you say?'

Juli shot me a furious look. 'They're not getting a cent from me,' she hissed.

Erik backed me up. 'I don't think that's a bad idea at all,' he said. 'So how about it then?'

Felix and Leander turned their backs on us and conferred in whispers, heads together. 'We accept your offer,' Felix said after a short while. 'Under one condition,' he then added with a bashful smile. 'You tell them, Leander.'

His friend smoothed his hair back from his pimply forehead and nodded at Juli. 'We want to see her naked again.'

Juli sounded like she was choking on her own laughter.

'Listen, guys,' said Paul, struggling to keep his voice under control, 'that's just not going to happen.'

'Pity,' said Felix. 'In that case, I'm afraid we'll have to insist on the full two hundred euros.'

'OK, I've had enough of this. Who do you think you are anyway?' Juli took two quick steps towards Felix, who shrank back in shock. 'FUCK – OFF!' she bellowed in his face.

Corky growled. Out of the corner of my eye, I saw him hobble forwards, and before I could call him back, he had already clamped his jaws on to Felix's trouser leg. Leander gripped his baseball bat with both hands and raised it over his head.

And that's when it all kicked off. Images flashed through my mind in rapid succession.

Me diving on to Leander and trying to wrestle the bat from his hands. Erik and Paul grabbing Felix and forcing him to the ground. Juli calling Corky to heel . . .

Then a loud crack catapulted me back to reality as Corky's skull shattered under the force of Leander's blow. The dog's jaws fell slack and he let go of Felix with a single heartrending whimper. A tremor passed through his body and his legs buckled beneath him. Juli uttered a piercing scream and I looked away, clamping both hands to my mouth and gagging on the bile rising in my throat.

'Thanks, Leander,' Felix said to his friend. 'That was close.'

'You're very welcome,' Leander replied in his silky soft voice.

6

'Hello? Are you still there?'

Toni's voice emerges tinnily from the handset on the floor. I bend down and reach out for it, only to jerk my hand back.

'Hello? Michaela?'

I'm powerless to respond, staring at the dark lump of plastic as if it's a dangerous animal that might spring to life at any second and pounce on me. I hear Toni call my name a few more times and then it goes quiet. She's obviously given up and ended the call.

A rush of adrenaline releases me from my state of shock. Every single one of my nerves feels like it's vibrating and I can't seem to get my thoughts straight. Two words run through my mind on an endless loop.

It's him.

I snatch my coat from the rack, drag it on and dash out of the apartment. It's only when I'm standing outside on the wet pavement that I realise I'm still in my pyjamas and slippers, so I whirl round, hurry back upstairs and throw on some clothes. I get such a shock when the phone rings, it gives me palpitations. It has to be Toni ringing back. I rush out of the door again and keep up the same rapid pace all the way to the S-Bahn station, my brain working on overdrive. Suddenly it occurs to me that the man in the stairwell last night had to be Toni's husband, David. He must have called her on his way up to let her know he was nearly home, and my ears must have converted the words *Toni darling* into *Maike darling*.

It takes forever for a train to arrive, and by the time I reach the bookshop, I'm in a complete state. Luckily there aren't any customers around. My mother has her back to the entrance and seems to be searching for something on one of the shelves. She turns round when the bell over the door jingles to announce my arrival.

'What are you doing here? It's your day off!' She looks at me in surprise.

I can't speak – I just stand and stare at her.

'Has something happened?' she asks anxiously.

'Yes. No. Not exactly,' I gabble. 'I know who he is. I recognised his voice and—'

I notice my mother's expression instantly shift as concern gives way to disapproval.

'Please, honey,' she says, 'not this again.'

'I'm absolutely positive this time.'

'Just like you were every other time.'

'But I—'

'No!' she says, cutting me off sharply; that's not like her at all. 'You have to stop with all these hunches of yours. You've caused enough trouble already. Last time you accused one of our customers, remember?'

I go red and lower my eyes in shame.

How could I have forgotten? It happened last August. I was in the kitchen, my mum was serving a customer out front in the shop, and when I heard his voice, my mug slipped from my hand and shattered on the floor. It was like an electric shock. I peeled back the curtain between the front and back rooms and peered through. The customer had his back to me. He was a blond, rangy man and he spoke with the exact same voice as Leander. I shrank back,

51

scarcely daring to breathe, but when the bell rang as he opened the door to leave, I sprang into action. Without stopping to think, I dashed past my mother and out on to the street. I could see her baffled expression out of the corner of my eye as I hurtled through the shop, my body prickling with agitation. I followed the guy into the inner courtyard of an apartment block and watched him unlock the door to a ground-floor flat. Next to the doorbell was a sign saying *L. & S. Scherer*. The *L.* stood for Leander – that seemed immediately obvious to me. I had tracked him down at long last. I pulled out my phone and called the police.

What happened next was so embarrassing that, looking back, I wish I could scrub it from my memory. After a half-hour wait that felt like an eternity, two police officers arrived on the scene. Breathlessly I told them what I'd seen and the conclusions I'd come to. They looked at me sceptically, had a muttered conversation and then rang the doorbell. The whole thing quickly turned out to be a mistake on my part. The *L.* stood for Ludwig, not Leander. Herr Scherer was a primary-school teacher and a single father, and his age alone ruled him out. He was nearly fifty. The upshot of the whole thing was that the police officers made me apologise to him and then took me back to the station. It wasn't the first time I'd made a false accusation, so I didn't exactly get the warmest of welcomes.

Mum walks up to me, gives me a hug and strokes my face tenderly. 'Darling, can't you see you're just going round and round in circles?' Her voice has recovered its usual warmth. 'You're only hurting yourself with all this. You need to draw a line under it, once and for all. It happened over fifteen years ago now.' She says the number with special emphasis. 'Let it go. Please?'

Biting my lower lip, I nod.

She tips my chin with her index finger. My eyes well up, splintering her face into tiny blurred fragments.

'Promise me you won't go to the police this time,' she says.

I give another nod, fighting back my tears.

Behind me, I hear the jingle of the bell and a waft of cold air washes over me. Mum gives me an apologetic look and shifts her attention to the customer who's just come in.

'Good morning! Can I help you at all or are you just browsing?'

I turn to leave without waiting to hear the reply, but Mum hangs on to my arm and gives me a searching look.

'Come over tonight and tell me all about it, OK?' She already seems to regret having spoken to me so bluntly earlier.

'It's fine,' I mutter. 'Forget it. I was probably overreacting.'

I can tell she doesn't quite believe me, but I give her a quick peck on the cheek and leave the shop.

Out on the street, I'm not sure what to do with myself. I don't feel like going home – I'm still too restless and agitated – but my feet carry me towards the S-Bahn station nonetheless.

I can't go to the police. That much is obvious, even without my mother's warning. They're not going to take me seriously after that last incident with the teacher. But what if I'm right this time? What should I do? I need to know for sure. This time, I need hard evidence that I've got the right man. Only when I have that can I go to the police, and not before. The first thing I need to do is get a proper look at Toni's husband. If he really is Leander, I'll recognise him.

Less than half an hour later, I'm standing outside Toni's building. The wind is like a cold breath playing over my face. My finger is hovering over the doorbell, but then panic suddenly washes over me at the idea of coming face to face with David. What will I do if he does turn out to be Leander? Should I accuse him directly? He'll only deny it. Feign incomprehension. Of course he will. And I still won't have a shred of evidence against him.

I take my hand away from the bell. Crazy idea. This is going to get me nowhere fast. I need to think. What I really need is a plan – a carefully thought-out plan. I turn on my heel and leave, almost stumbling over my feet in my haste to get away. As I walk back to the S-Bahn station, I notice a few spots of rain. Within seconds, water is gushing from the sky and I take shelter in a small café, where I'm enveloped in a loud hubbub of people chatting and laughing. The scent of freshly baked bread and hot coffee fills my nose, my empty stomach starts to rumble, and on a whim, I decide to treat myself to breakfast. The place is packed, but I spot an empty table by the window and hurry over before anyone else can claim it. I throw my coat on the back of a chair, sit down, push the previous customers' dirty crockery to one side and reach for the menu. It's plastic and feels sticky to the touch. Gingerly, I leaf through the laminated pages. A stick-thin waitress dressed head to toe in black with a grey-white bob grumpily takes my order. I almost have to shout to make myself heard over the noise of the coffee machine and the buzz of conversation from the neighbouring tables.

'I'll bring the cappuccino right away, but the breakfast will take a while.' She nods towards the other tables. 'You can see what we're up against.'

I assure her that it's fine, then lean back and look around the room. Realising I'm the only person here on my own, I instantly feel out of place, not sure what to do with my hands. I have the strongest urge to get up and leave, but force myself to stay put. I need to learn not to run away from every uncomfortable situation. My therapist has been drumming that into me for years now. So I pull my phone out of my pocket – only to notice, to my surprise, that I have two missed calls. Barely anyone ever calls me, apart from my mother. One is from Toni, and the other is a number I don't recognise. Should I call Toni back? Not now. Later. I don't want to make any more rash decisions.

The waitress returns to my table holding a full tray and wordlessly deposits a cappuccino in front of me. I put my phone away and lift the cup to my lips. Just then, the door to the café opens to the latest two arrivals. Shaking their rain-slicked umbrellas, they scan the room, and I almost choke on my coffee.

It's Toni – accompanied by a man. David? Probably. I shrink down in my seat, as if I could hide behind my cup, but Toni's already spotted me. Her face lights up. She waves, says something to the man beside her and then waddles towards me between the tables at surprising speed.

'Toni,' I say, 'what a lovely surprise.'

It sounds feeble and far from enthusiastic, but she doesn't seem to notice. She pulls up an empty chair from the neighbouring table and waves her companion over. My pulse quickens; I can't bring myself to look at him. With a loud sigh, Toni unwinds the scarf from around her neck.

'Such godawful weather,' she says, lowering herself into the chair opposite. 'So what happened this morning? You suddenly went quiet on the phone.'

'No idea,' I trot out in reply, blushing at the outright lie. 'The phone just went dead. It's been happening a lot lately.'

'Tell me about it,' says Toni, rolling her eyes. 'This is David, by the way.' She gestures to the man now sitting next to her. 'David, this is Michaela, an old schoolfriend of mine. We bumped into each other the other day. When was it again? The day before yesterday?'

She chatters on cheerfully. I haven't taken my eyes off Toni since she got here, but I can't follow a word of what she's saying. I can feel David's eyes resting on me, making me more anxious by the second.

Is he wondering where he knows me from?

'Hi,' he says, once Toni has finished her speech, and gives me his hand across the table. I reach out mechanically and shake it, still avoiding looking him in the face.

'It's so nice to meet you at last,' he adds in Leander's soft voice.

I swallow and my body goes hot and then cold. The blood drains from my head into my belly. Toni raises her eyebrows and looks at me intently. She says something, but I don't hear a word.

I'm staring at David. At the acne scars on his cheeks and his smooth, straw-coloured hair, which he brushes back from his forehead with an impatient gesture. His ice-grey eyes lock with mine, and David's face dissolves into a blur. I blink as I bring it back into focus, but then the shock comes like a punch to the stomach. Leander is sitting opposite me, his cheeks and forehead covered in red pustules, a baseball bat slung over his shoulder. His lips move soundlessly. *Maike darling?* I push my chair back.

'Excuse me,' I just about manage to croak. Then I get up, grab my bag and stumble to the lavatory, where, hunched over the toilet bowl, my stomach heaves out its contents in a violent gush. I retch until there's nothing left but bile and then stagger to my feet with a groan. I hardly recognise the ashen figure looking back at me from the mirror over the sink. Horror is etched into my face.

You need to pull yourself together. You can't let them see that there's anything wrong.

I turn on the tap and drink water from my cupped hands to wash the revolting taste from my mouth. *How am I supposed to face them both like everything's just fine?* I ask my reflection. I can't see how it's possible. But it's time I went back to the table – I've spent far too long in here already and Toni's bound to come and check on me before long. The best thing would be to pay at the counter, pick up my coat and make my excuses. Tell them I'm not feeling very well. Anyone would believe that, given how pale I look right now. I take a deep breath and head back out into the café.

But the chairs at the table are empty. I peer around the room. No sign of Toni or David. But instead of relief that I don't have to face them, an uneasy feeling comes over me. Did David recognise me and decide to make himself scarce? Hesitantly I sit back down. The skinny waitress shuffles past and plonks my breakfast on the table in front of me.

'Your friends asked me to tell you that they had to leave unexpectedly,' she says.

'Did they say why?'

'Nope,' comes the curt reply.

How odd. It really does seem like they ran away. I ask for the bill, pushing the plate laden with sliced sausage, cheese, tomatoes, bread and jam to one side with a grimace. My appetite is well and truly gone.

Quiet doubts gnaw at me on the way home. There could be any number of reasons why they both left so abruptly. It doesn't necessarily have anything to do with me. And I don't have any proof that David is Leander. I only know one thing for certain: David's voice is uncannily similar to Leander's. But as my mother so clearly reminded me, this isn't the first time I've heard someone who sounded like him. Certain men's voices have a particular tone that triggers something in me, my therapist explained. The images they call up might not even be real – they might only exist in my head.

I prowl restlessly through the rooms of my apartment, moving books back and forth, dusting the furniture and peering out of the window. David's voice won't leave me; it rings incessantly in my ear. I rub my neck, which is aching from all the strain. What should I do now? However much I rack my brain, I can't come up with any way to confirm my suspicions. It'd be better to drop the whole thing – but the moment the idea runs through my mind, I realise

I can't. Not anymore. First I need to make certain that David isn't Leander. There'll be no peace for me otherwise.

◆ ◆ ◆

The next day goes by like I'm watching a film. I'm on autopilot, my brain completely switched off. *Whatever you do, don't think.* Toni doesn't get in touch. Just as well, as I still don't know what I should say to her. I do, however, get a call from Alexander.

'Toni was kind enough to give me your mobile number. I tried ringing earlier, but there was no reply,' he says, before apologising for his sudden departure the other night.

'No worries,' I assure him.

When he asks if I fancy going for coffee, I reply, 'That'd be great.' I'm not actually sure if it's such a good idea but I don't want to give him the cold shoulder again. We arrange to meet the evening after tomorrow.

My mother, who was eavesdropping on the conversation, gives me a conspiratorial wink. I've told her that I met Alexander at the party and unexpectedly clicked with him. Now that he's called, she'll almost certainly suspect something might be brewing between us. I wave her away, feeling myself blush, and Mum draws her lips into a knowing smile. I open my mouth to disabuse her, but then I decide to let her believe what she wants. She would so love to see me with a man by my side at long last. As if that would solve all my problems.

7

Another day goes by, and I'm unable to shake the feeling that I'm standing outside my own body, coolly watching everything I do. Feigning a cold, I call Alexander to cancel and promise to get in touch as soon as I'm better.

At night, I lie awake, David's voice continuously forcing its way into my mind. His soft sing-song voice has become a constant presence and I hear him saying, 'It's so nice to meet you at last,' over and over until I start to feel like my skull is about to explode.

The following day, after a stressful morning in the bookshop, I'm about to take a late lunch when Toni WhatsApps me a photo of her looking exhausted but very happy, cradling her newborn son in her arms. Underneath it, she writes:

Introducing Leander, our little ray of sunshine.

An ice-cold chill runs through my body. Clutching my phone, I stagger over and slump on to the sofa. Leander? Can that be a coincidence? It's hardly a common name these days. The arrival of a second message interrupts my thoughts.

He came a little early, which is why we left the café in such a hurry the other day. We're both staying in hospital

for another week. Will you come and visit? I'm at the
maternity clinic in Schöneberg. Toni XX (over the moon!)

I run over to Mum with my phone.

'Toni's had her baby. Guess what they've called it.'

'How on earth should I know, sweetheart?' She rolls her eyes in a show of exasperation. 'Is it a boy or a girl?'

'A boy,' I reply.

'Oh yes – we wondered about that, didn't we?'

'They've called him' – I pause for effect – 'Leander.' Then I fix her with a meaningful look.

'Should we send her some flowers? Or are you going to visit?'

My mother can be very slow on the uptake at times.

'Mum, they're calling the baby *Leander*!'

She lifts her eyebrows in surprise. 'What's so significant about . . . ?' Then she catches herself and frowns as she finally puts two and two together. 'Oh! You think—?'

'Exactly,' I cut in. 'It can't be a coincidence.'

'And I suppose Toni's husband is the man whose voice you think you've recognised?' She gives me a searching look, her eyes narrowed to slits.

'Precisely.' I nod eagerly. 'And now this. It can't be a coincidence,' I add, emphasising my point through repetition.

'Oh yes, it can. And that's exactly what it is – a coincidence,' Mum replies in a tone that brooks no disagreement. 'Just give this a rest now, OK? Toni's your friend – and yet you suspect her husband of committing a horrible crime? Stop and think for a second. How many times have you already mistaken some poor innocent man for Leander? You can't go on doing this. I don't want to hear another word about these groundless suspicions of yours. Have I made myself clear?'

I've rarely seen my mother as worked up as she is now. She turns on her heel and disappears into the back room, leaving me feeling like a scolded child. Defiance rears up in me, more so now than ever before. I'm going to prove to her that I'm right.

I spend the rest of the day feeling oddly euphoric. An idea steals into my mind – insane, foolhardy and probably unworkable, but I can't stop thinking about it. What do I have to lose?

I wait until I get home before I reply to Toni's message. I've thought carefully about what I want to say.

> *Congratulations, Toni! I'm so happy for you. It's a lovely name, but an unusual one too. Not one you come across very often these days. Love, Michaela*

The reply comes through a few seconds later.

> *Thank you! The name was David's idea. Apparently it's something to do with a Greek myth he was obsessed with when he was a boy. It took him a while to convince me, what with it being so old-fashioned and everything, but now I think it's beautiful – just like my little treasure. XX*

I stare at the message until the display fades to black. A Greek myth? I'm guessing she means Hero and Leander, and vaguely recall the tale of a star-crossed couple who met a tragic end. On the surface, David's explanation seems entirely reasonable, but it's the missing piece of the puzzle – the last detail I needed to confirm my suspicions once and for all. David is Leander.

My knees go weak. I stumble over to the dining table and sit down heavily. I'm trembling from head to foot, but my mind's made up.

I'm going to make David confess to what he's done. And I know just how to do it. It's not going to be easy. My plan may not work out. It could even be dangerous. But I'm willing to take the risk. I have to – I owe it to myself and my friends.

2003

'He's dead. Corky's dead.' Juli's voice was little more than a murmur.

I gulped. My head was spinning. I knew my phone was in my backpack, which was next to my bike, just a few steps away. But what good would it do if I managed to get to it? Even if I had any signal out here, which I doubted, I didn't know where we were. Somewhere in Brandenburg by a lake – that was all. I racked my brains for the name of the sleepy village we'd stopped in earlier to pick up a few supplies for tonight. Was it Marienwalde? Liebkirchen? I couldn't quite remember.

'Maybe we should go now,' said Felix. His eyes were still fixed on Juli, who was crouching beside her dead dog and sobbing her heart out.

Leander rested his baseball bat on his shoulder. I felt a wave of revulsion at the sight of the thick blood clinging to the wood. 'What about our money though?' he insisted. 'I mean, yes, the dog's dead, but we still brought him back for you.'

'Of course!' Felix struck his forehead with the flat of his hand. 'Thank you for reminding me. I would have completely forgotten otherwise.' He turned to Paul and Erik. 'So, what about our money?'

Juli suddenly leaped to her feet and hurled herself at Felix with a shriek. She laid into him with both hands, her face slick with tears.

'You fucking murderers!' she screamed. 'You'll pay for this. I'm going to put you behind bars.'

Felix gave Juli a powerful shove and she stumbled and fell flat on her back. Laughing, he held up his hands as if this was all just a game and cried, 'All right, I give in!'

Still snivelling, Juli struggled to her feet and wiped her nose on the back of her hand before launching herself at him again and pummelling him with her fists. Leander stood to one side with his bat still slung over his shoulder. He didn't take his eyes off the rest of us for a second, and I knew he wouldn't hesitate to use it if anyone else moved.

'Juli, please. Stop,' I begged her. 'This isn't helping.'

Felix threw his arms around Juli and clamped her in a bear hug before looking across at his friend. 'Ooh, her nipples have gone hard.'

His mocking grin sent a shudder down my spine. Juli spat in his face. Felix let her go, bunched his fist and punched her right in the face.

Once.

Twice.

Juli tottered on her feet, her head slung to one side.

The third punch landed on her temple and she silently toppled over, hitting the ground hard, blood trickling from her ear.

I screamed, threw my hands over my mouth and drew back a step. My ears were buzzing. Paul and Erik just stood there as if they were paralysed with shock.

'Dear oh dear, why on earth are you making this so difficult for us?' Felix complained as he took out his bloodstained handkerchief and languidly wiped the saliva from his face.

Erik rummaged in his pockets and pulled out a crumpled fifty-euro note. 'Here, this is all I have,' he said. He took a step towards Felix and held the note out to him. His fingers were trembling.

Felix plucked it from Erik's hand and passed it to Leander, who examined both sides and then tossed it away. It fluttered through the air, coming to rest beside Juli's fingers. Out of the corner of my eye, I could see Paul clenching his fists.

'Now, was it really worth all this fuss?' said Leander, breaking the silence.

Maybe it was the priggish note in his voice that really got to Paul and Erik, but whatever the reason, the pair of them leaped forwards as if on command. Erik uttered a cry like that of a wounded animal. Felix raised his hand; I caught a glimpse of dull metal and heard an ominous click. Leander dragged his baseball bat off his shoulder and gripped it in both hands.

In that same split-second, I decided to make a run for it. Whirling around, I sprang over the dead dog and fled from the scene. The blood-red ball of the setting sun glowed just over the treetops. My friends' screams pursued me deep into the forest, punctuated by loud bangs that reverberated through the trees. I stopped only when the stitch in my side grew unbearable and bent over, bracing myself with my hands on my knees, my lungs burning. I had no clue where I was. Guilty thoughts tickled at the back of my mind, but I quickly hushed them. There was nothing I could have done against those two. Someone needed to get help. It was our only chance. Taking a deep breath, I dashed onwards, parting the vegetation with both hands as it grew ever thicker. My bare arms and legs were scratched and bleeding from the thorns, but I barely registered the pain as I pounded on through the forest with grim determination. Time and again I stumbled, fell, but then staggered back to my feet. I was utterly exhausted and every step was excruciating. At one point, a bird shot up from the undergrowth right in front of me, scaring me half to death.

Then, to my surprise, I emerged on to a footpath, where I broke down in tears of sheer relief. I hesitated in the middle of the track, my eyes flicking to right and then left. My gut instinct told me to go right, but I didn't trust myself when it came to navigation, so I wiped away my tears and headed left – only to come to a halt after a few yards and turn back. The path seemed to stretch on forever. My legs ached, my feet throbbed and I was tormented by thirst. I had to force myself to put one foot in front of the other.

At last the path curved and grew wider, and the forest cleared. I staggered to a halt and stared in disbelief. The dark waters of a lake stretched out in front of me below the pale light of the rising moon. It took a few seconds to grasp what I'd done. I'd gone in a huge circle.

This time, I pushed down the urge to run and ducked behind a bush, before peering out along the shoreline. And there everything was – the tents, the dead dog, our bikes – exactly where we'd left it all. It seemed an eternity since I'd last been here. I'd lost all track of time in my headlong rush to get away.

But where were the others? I couldn't see any sign of them. Had they managed to escape? Reluctantly I emerged from the safety of my hiding place, trembling from head to toe with a sudden rush of adrenaline. Crouching down and constantly scanning my surroundings, I scurried towards the bikes, but disappointment hit me like a punch in the gut. The tyres were all flat. Someone had slashed them.

My eyes fell on a bare foot poking out from one of the tents. I rushed over and bent down, then lifted the door flap to one side, but my mind refused to process the scene inside. Bile burned in my throat, making me gag, and I had to struggle not to throw up.

Juli was lying on her side, her long dark hair covering her face and torso. Beside her lay Paul, blood oozing from a gaping wound in his chest, his eyes fixed unseeing on the roof of the tent. Erik was sprawled next to him, his eyes closed. It looked like someone had thrown a bucket of blood over him.

With a sob, I fell to my knees in the blood that had soaked through the roll mats and was now lying in thick puddles on the plastic floor of the tent. I whispered my friends' names over and over, even though I knew they couldn't hear me.

A noise behind me made me scramble back to my feet. On the shore of the lake, I could make out the dim outline of two figures. They spotted me too in the same moment. Peering through the darkness, I could see one of them had something in his hand. Was it the baseball bat? He pointed towards me and the two of them started marching in my direction. With a loud sob, I took off again, tears streaming from my eyes, clouding my vision. Half blind, I stumbled back into the woods, where I tripped over something on the ground and landed flat on my face. The wind carried a voice to my ear, soft as silk, as if calling to a timid cat.

'Maike darling.'

My breath caught.

'Maike darling, where are you?'

I scrambled back to my feet and hurried onwards, keeping low to the ground. Dead ahead, a figure emerged from the dark grey shadows of the woods and lunged towards me.

'Ah, there you are!'

Felix.

He came to a stop a couple of feet in front of me and his mouth twisted into a grin that flooded me with panic.

I shrank back. Felix stayed still, the same false smile on his face. I took another step back, only to bump into something. I whirled around, my heart pounding like a jackhammer. Leander. He stood

66

there, staring down at me as if carved out of stone, his face a complete blank except for the malicious glint in his eye.

'We were so worried we'd lost you,' he said with a sickening warmth.

My eyes flicked back and forth between them. 'Why are you doing this?' My question came out as little more than a squeak.

Felix pouted, gazed helplessly across at his friend and shrugged his shoulders. 'I don't know, Leander – why *are* we doing this?'

'Maybe . . .' Leander began, before pausing as if to think hard about what he might say next. 'Maybe . . . because we're evil, Felix?'

The two of them grinned at each other over my head. I felt sick to my stomach. The ground began to sway beneath my feet and then gave way altogether. I fell. Two hands lifted me up by the armpits and started to drag me, my feet bumping along the ground. I opened my mouth and screamed for help as loud as I could, but my voice cracked.

When I did that, they dropped me – so fast that my face hit the ground hard. I heard a loud crack, like a dog biting through a bone, and could taste the musty reek of the forest floor. Then a searing pain shot through me, nearly robbing me of my senses. A hand grabbed my hair and dragged me to my feet. I screamed again, loud and piercing this time, and Felix smashed his fist into my face. Pain exploded in my head. Red spots flickered in front of my eyes and everything went black.

When I came to, I was strapped to a tree with a gag in my mouth. Breathing through my nose was agony – they must have broken it. I struggled to get enough air. Gradually my eyes adjusted to the dark. The trunks of the trees stood in serried ranks and seemed to be watching me, like a line of mute soldiers.

I couldn't see Felix or Leander, but could feel their presence with every fibre of my being. Then I heard a quiet chuckle that chilled me to the marrow.

'You're in luck,' I heard Felix say. 'Isn't she, Leander?'

'Very much so,' Leander replied in his silky soft voice. 'We're far too generous for our own good, Felix.'

'That we are,' the other boy confirmed.

'We're going to let you live.'

'Take care now, Maike,' Felix said.

Their footsteps faded away.

Terror welled up inside me.

You can't do this! my voice roared in my head, though not a sound came past my lips.

8

'A holiday? Now, of all times?' My mother is staring at me with such dismay that my guilty conscience flares up like a blowtorch and I find myself on the verge of taking back my request.

'Please. Just those two days. It's the only time Alexander can get away,' I plead, feeling another surge of guilt at lying to her. I've led her to believe that Alexander and I went on a date and hit it off. That seemed like the most plausible excuse. 'The Christmas season doesn't really get going until next week.'

She frowns and purses her lips, but I can tell she's wavering.

'Please,' I say again.

'All right, fine. Just this once,' she says with a theatrical sigh, but she's smiling too.

'Thank you.' I throw my arms around her neck. 'You're so good to me.'

She hugs me back and plants a damp kiss on my cheek. 'So where are you and Alexander off to then?'

'He hasn't said,' I reply. 'It's meant to be a surprise.'

'Well, I hope it's fun, darling. Have a wonderful time. You truly deserve it.'

My cheeks glow hot with shame. Turning my face aside, I rush out of the shop. On the way home, however, my guilty conscience gives way to anxiety. Again and again, I run over every stage of my plan in my mind, telling myself that I've gone over every last detail and nothing can possibly go wrong.

My elderly Ford has had a 'For Sale' sign stuck to the windscreen for the past few months, but I'm glad now it hasn't found a buyer. I drive to the post office and buy the biggest cardboard box they have. Then I head to a DIY shop, where I stock up on bricks and headtorches. I've already ordered the taser, chloroform and everything else on my list online from the computer in the bookshop, and it all arrived this morning via express delivery. And it was equally straightforward looking up the exact co-ordinates of my destination. Three cheers for the Internet, eh?

Last of all, I retrieve my father's gun from the drawer of my bedside table and tuck it into my backpack along with all my new purchases. Then I go through the list again to make sure I've not forgotten anything. My whole body is twitching with anticipation. I slip into my thick down jacket, pull on my fur-lined boots and shut the apartment door behind me. The lock catches with a quiet click. A melancholy settles over me as I realise that I've arrived at a turning point in my life. By the time I come home, things will be very different.

The weather's got a little warmer over the last few days, so I quickly overheat in my thick coat. I shove my heavily laden backpack in the boot of my car and walk over to a nearby payphone. My hand trembles as I dial the number. After three rings, someone picks up.

'Hello?'

I instantly hang up. He's there – that's all I need to know. I can get to work. I hurry back to the car and then drive five minutes up the road, where I park in front of a Turkish grocery store. The narrow side street is deserted at this time of day, which is exactly why I picked it.

Instead of hopping out of the car, I remain seated at the wheel. It's already getting dark. As if on command, the streetlights come on. Their pale glow makes the bare trees at the side of the road appear like frozen giants, waving their long arms. My heart is pounding. *Breathe*, I urge myself silently. But I can't seem to catch my breath over my mounting panic.

How should I react if he does something unexpected? What if he recognised me as the girl from the lake? What if he's been waiting for an opportunity like this all along? He might drag me into his apartment and murder me. I shrink back into my car seat.

By now the windscreen is completely clouded over from my breath and the heat from my body. Only a vague glow from the streetlights filters into the car. Fear has settled in a hard lump in the pit of my stomach.

I mustn't give in. With growing resolve now, I get out of the car, open the boot, and tuck the taser and everything else I need in my coat pocket. I pull my hood up and wrap a scarf around my neck. At the last minute, I remember to push the passenger seat all the way forwards. Then I lock up the car and head off.

A few minutes later, I find myself outside the building on Skalitzer Strasse, where I press the bell for one of the top-floor flats. The door buzzes open without anyone even asking over the intercom who might be down here. The stairwell reeks of a pungent blend of frying bacon and cat piss. The throbbing bass and howling guitars of somebody's rock music is blasting out at top volume from one of the upper storeys. A sign on the lift says, 'OUT OF ORDER'. Slowly I climb the stairs, fighting nausea all the way. I'm so agitated that I'm not sure I'll be able to string two words together. Up at the third floor, I take a few deep breaths, plaster a smile on my face and ring the doorbell.

It takes a while before I hear the sound of footsteps approaching, and then the door swings open. I've been steeling myself for this moment and thought I was ready, but the sight of him comes like a smack in the face. I really have to force myself not to shrink back. From the sudden flash in his ice-grey eyes, I know he recognises me.

'Yes?' He folds his arms over his chest and plants himself firmly in the doorway. His whole body is signalling that I'm not welcome here.

'Hello, David,' I say, hoping he won't notice the shaky undertone to my voice. 'I'm a friend of Toni's – we met in the café across the road the other day?'

'Yes, I remember.' David remains where he is, his face a blank, and makes no sign of asking me in.

He's cool and dismissive, in sharp contrast to the politeness with which he greeted me in the café. Was that because Toni was there with him? Did he put on a front for her sake?

'I just wanted to say congratulations. Toni sent me a photo of your new baby.' I force a smile. 'He's very cute.'

'Thanks,' he replies curtly.

'I don't want to keep you for long,' I add quickly. 'I've just brought you a gift to celebrate the new arrival – only the thing is, it's really heavy, and about this big.' Pursing my lips, I sketch out the size with my hands. 'The lift's out of order and I can't bring it up on my own. Do you reckon you could give me a hand? My car's just around the corner – about two minutes' walk.' I grow more breathless with every word and barely manage to get that last sentence out at all.

David raises his eyebrows and wrinkles appear on his brow. *Say yes*, I implore him silently, *please say yes*. I smile as broadly as I can.

'This is kind of a bad time,' he replies, without a trace of regret, and brushes a lock of hair from his face.

'That's a shame,' I say. 'It's just that I'm going away for a few days. But if now doesn't work for you . . .' I shrug. My disappointment comes mingled with a vague sense of relief. If he's not going to play ball, there's precious little I can do about it.

'Sorry, but I'm right in the middle of something,' he says.

'Hey, no problem,' I reply as casually as I can. 'I'll come again when Toni's back home. Sorry to bother you. Have a nice evening.' I turn to leave.

'Oh what the hell,' I hear him say behind me. 'Wait a sec – let me just get my coat.'

'Thanks,' I say automatically and linger in the corridor, unsure whether I should be pleased about this sudden change of heart. The palms of my hands are sweating. I don't know if I'm ready.

'OK, I'm ready.'

His voice startles me, cutting into the silence like an echo of my thoughts.

We walk to my car without another word. I'm more and more tense with every step, but more and more determined too. I steal a glance at David. He's not wearing a scarf, just a thin coat. That's good. Perfect, in fact.

'Here we are,' I say when we arrive at my car. My mouth is so dry, it's a struggle to get the words out. The car key slips through my fingers, but David picks it up and hands it to me.

'The present is on the back seat.' I take the key without acknowledging his gesture. 'It's a real pain but the door's jammed on the left, so you'll have to go in from this side.' I open the right-hand door for him.

He bends down and leans into the car. I push my hand into my pocket and grip the taser. David reaches out, but can't quite get a grip on the box, just as I'd hoped.

'Come on, you bloody thing,' he mutters, shooting a withering look over his shoulder at me that I answer with a shrug and a smile of apology.

He plants his knees on the seat. I look up and down the road. Not a soul to be seen.

'What have you got in there?' he asks, trying to draw the box towards him with both hands. 'Bricks or something?' He doesn't know it but he's hit the nail on the proverbial head.

'Wait, let me help you,' I say and squeeze in alongside him.

Before he can react, I hold the taser to his throat and press the button. It sparks into life with an appalling crackle, like hair going up in flames. My whole body is shaking; I offer up a silent prayer that no one happens to walk past right now. David's face twists into a grimace and he screams. I wasn't expecting that. I'm suddenly flooded with adrenaline and press the device even harder against his neck, glancing anxiously out at the street, but the windows are still fogged over and I can't see a thing.

It takes a while, but David eventually falls silent. Ten seconds, according to the manual, and then the taser switches off automatically. With my free hand, I fumble for the duct tape I've left on the tray between the two front seats. I'm just slipping the roll over my wrist like a bracelet when the taser cuts out. I throw it on the floor and then wrap tape round David's ankles. I need to move fast while he's still paralysed from the shock. His body is in a foetal position on the back seat with his legs in the footwell and his head propped against the box. There's drool trickling from the corner of his mouth. I yank his arms behind his back and wrap his wrists in several loops of tape. Then I curse myself. How could I forget the chloroform? I fumble in my inner pocket for the bottle and a handkerchief, which I soak with the fluid before clamping it over David's nose and mouth. He gives a muffled cry and then his whole body twitches as if he's having some sort of seizure. After what seems like an eternity, his body finally goes limp.

By the time I clamber back out of the car, I'm stiff all over and drenched in sweat. I shove David's feet inside, slam the door and wipe the moisture from my forehead with the back of my hand. It's done.

'What are you doing?' asks a voice.

I freeze.

9

I turn round as if in slow motion. A small boy in a woolly hat, his cheeks rosy from the cold, is trying to see past me through the car window; he can't be any more than seven or eight. I dart to the side to block his view.

'Where's your mother?' I ask in my sternest voice.

'She's over with Grandad.' He waves a brown-mittened hand towards the other side of the road. 'Did you kill that man in there?' The boy's desperately craning his neck, trying to get a good look in.

Before I can come up with a suitable reply, I hear the clatter of high heels on tarmac. There's a woman hurrying across the street towards us.

'I'm so sorry.' She gives me a brief glance and then yanks the boy by the arm. 'How many times have I told you not to talk to strangers?' she scolds as she drags the child away.

'But, Mummy, that lady had a man in her—'

I walk around the car and climb into the driver's seat, before hastily stuffing the chloroform and taser into the glove compartment. In the rear-view mirror, I notice that the woman has stopped and is staring in my direction.

My hands grip the steering wheel. *Stay calm*. Somehow I manage to turn the key in the ignition and start the engine. As I pull out, I fail to spot an approaching car and nearly cause an accident.

Brakes squeal, a horn blares. I hold up my hand in apology and drive on. I need to get out of here. Leave the city behind.

Only now does it dawn on me quite how reckless that was. It could all have gone so horribly wrong. My plan was clearly not as watertight as I thought. My heart won't stop pounding.

I switch on the satnav, having already programmed the route last night. Unfortunately I can't get us all the way to our final destination by car; we'll have to cover the last stretch through the woods on foot. That's the part that worries me most.

It takes me around three quarters of an hour to get out of Berlin. As I drive down the motorway, a few droplets start to patter against the windscreen and, before I know it, rain is hammering on the roof like a machine gun. According to the digital reading on the dashboard, the temperature outside the car is three degrees Celsius. I hope it won't get any colder. Icy roads are the last thing I need right now. I can see David growing increasingly restless in the rear-view mirror. His head is tossing from side to side and he keeps grunting quietly to himself. He isn't fully awake yet, but the chloroform is bound to wear off before long. I put my foot down.

The wipers churn frantically back and forth across the windscreen. A lorry overtakes me and the spray engulfs the car, obscuring my view for a good few seconds. The motorway exit comes as a relief, and the satnav suggests we'll be there in another fifteen minutes or so. Dark walls of densely packed trees line the edges of the country road. The asphalt glistens with water and huge puddles have collected in the potholes.

The groans from my unwilling passenger on the backseat are getting more and more frequent. He's sure to wake up fully soon. With the restraints on his wrists and ankles, he doesn't pose a threat to me, but my heart beats faster all the same.

The rain stops as abruptly as it started and the female voice of the satnav cuts across the rumble of my battered old engine to inform me that my destination is six hundred yards off. Are we really there already? I lean over the steering wheel and peer through the windscreen. The surroundings look unfamiliar, though that's hardly a surprise. The last time I was here was over fifteen years ago, when the police brought me out to look at the crime scene. Wild horses couldn't drag me here after that, but I still remember a narrow path leading from the car park to the lake. Hopefully it hasn't grown over by now. That would be a problem.

'You have reached your destination,' my satnav announces, pulling me back to the present.

At the same moment, I spot the sign for the car park, and I turn off the road and pull up in one of the spaces. There are no other vehicles around. After a quick glance at David – eyes still closed, face twitching – I retrieve my torch from the glove compartment and get out of the car. The cold, damp air creeps under my clothing and my breath condenses into a cloud of vapour.

A car approaches along the road, its headlights on full beam. Shadows flicker along the ground. The lights pass over the leafless shrubs along the edge of the car park, making them look like a stack of bones. Behind them lies the impenetrable black of the forest. The car rushes past.

A rustling noise nearby, followed by a sharp crack. Is someone creeping around? I point the beam of my torch in the direction of the sound, but there's no one there. Obviously. All the same, the blood is throbbing in my temples. To my right, I spot the path. It's just a narrow gap through the trees, but it's still passable. A good omen.

I lift my backpack out of the boot and take out the two head-torches, then fit one of them to my head, switch it on and open the right-hand passenger door. David is awake; he turns his head and blinks into the light. His movements are strangely stiff and he's looking at me with a vacant expression. No sign of recognition.

But I recognise him all right – with a clarity that runs through my body like an electric shock, burning away any lingering doubts once and for all. The acne scars on his cheeks, the blond hair falling over his face. Those cold grey eyes.

David is the man who once called himself Leander. I've got the right one this time.

In my mind's eye, a film starts to play at high speed – one that started in this very car park in the summer of 2003. Back then I thought I was the happiest person alive. I was dating Paul. Michaela and Paul – I wanted to carve those words into the bark of a tree and frame them with a heart. But I never got the chance.

2003

It was warm and sunny, unusual even for mid-May. Paul and I were walking hand in hand along the narrow path, stopping every few yards to kiss. I was so in love, I felt like I might burst with happiness. There were times when I couldn't quite believe it – that he'd chosen me of all people to be his girlfriend. I had a constant need to touch him, to feel his body against mine, as if it was the only way to prove this wasn't a dream.

'This is a magical spot – our own special place,' he whispered in my ear when we arrived at a small lake, tucked away in a clearing in the woods.

He laid a woollen blanket on the sand by the shore of the lake and opened a bottle of champagne. He'd brought both items with him in his backpack. I never normally drank alcohol – wasn't too keen on the taste – but I didn't want to disappoint Paul. We took turns swigging from the bottle and I giggled each time the bubbles tickled my gums.

'You're so sweet, Michaela,' said Paul, pulling me in close.

Our kisses grew more passionate and I felt his warm hands slip under my T-shirt. He began to caress my breasts and I pressed my body up against him. I wanted him so badly it hurt.

'Is it your first time?' he whispered as he nudged my skirt up around my hips.

I nodded self-consciously.

'I'll be careful,' he murmured. His fingertips danced over my inner thighs. A wave of excitement rippled through my body and I moaned softly as his hand crept under my panties.

My whole body trembled and I could scarcely contain myself as Paul unzipped his fly and tugged at his jeans. Laughing, he let me go and peeled them off, while I quickly slipped off my underwear. Paul knelt over me and I lifted my hips towards him. Our eyes locked.

'I love you,' he whispered. Then he carefully entered me.

The pain was brief, but intense. I gritted my teeth. The first time always hurts – I knew that. Paul was panting now, his hips moving faster and faster. Suddenly he gave a single guttural moan and then collapsed on top of me. I was a little surprised that it was over so quickly. Paul's breath was hot against my neck. His body relaxed, draping itself over me, and my disappointment that it had been so short-lived gradually shifted into a feeling of tenderness. I ran my fingers through his sweaty hair and kissed him gently on the forehead. I'd never felt this close to anyone before in my life.

'I love you so much,' I whispered.

'Me too,' said Paul as he clambered to his feet.

I felt cold, and an odd feeling of something like shame welled up inside me. We dressed in silence and walked back to the car park. On the way, my euphoria gave way to anxiety. Had I done something wrong? I didn't dare ask. He seemed so unapproachable all of a sudden.

Paul drove me home, gave me a quick peck on the cheek and promised to call me. I waited and waited. Eventually I called him, but only ever got through to Juli, who just kept telling me her brother wasn't around.

Two days after that, I saw him holding hands with Maike after school. I was stunned. He'd told me he'd broken up with her because he was in love with me. I decided to confront him and started marching towards them, but then lost my nerve when I saw his cold glare.

Later, one of my classmates told me that Paul had been bragging at a party about how he could get his leg over any girl he wanted. She didn't know how much he and the others had bet on it; all she knew was that they'd settled on me as the target. The story had no doubt gone round the whole school already and I expect everyone was laughing at me behind my back.

Paul had used me. Little by little, the realisation trickled into my brain. I wanted to hate him but I couldn't. Maybe he had fallen in love with me after all and couldn't admit it for some reason. I nurtured a quiet but tenacious hope that this was all one big misunderstanding. It was like a tiny glimmer of light that refused to be extinguished.

The hatred didn't come until much later.

10

The sound of my phone ringing jolts me straight back into the present and I reach automatically into the pocket of my coat. It has to be my mother. Barely anyone calls me other than her, and she's the last person I want to talk to right now. She'd know right away something was up. A glance at the display confirms my suspicion. I ignore the call and stuff the phone back in my pocket.

'Out!' I order David.

He doesn't move, just stares at me. Is that fear in his eyes, or is he still out of it? I pull the gun from my backpack, point it at him and repeat my order.

Never once taking his eyes off me, he shuffles along the back seat to the door and lifts his legs out of the car. I have to steel myself before I'm able to grab his arm and help him out. He stands beside the open door, swaying slightly. Out of an abundance of caution, I take a couple of steps back.

'On your knees!'

He tries to do as I say, but only manages to bend awkwardly.

'I can't get any lower,' he says in a strained voice, 'because of the tape.'

'Stay like that then.' I tuck the gun into my coat pocket, go round behind him and pull the second headtorch over his head. He flinches, but says nothing.

'OK, stand up.' I take out my gun again.

'What's this all about? What do you want from me?' He trails off into a coughing fit. I wait for him to compose himself.

'The summer of 2003,' I say in reply.

'The summer of 2003?' he repeats, a note of incomprehension in his voice.

'2003,' I confirm.

He throws me a quizzical look, but I can see the treacherous gleam in his eye. He knows exactly what I'm referring to.

'I have absolutely no idea what you're talking about,' he lies. His eyes flick back and forth over the dark car park as if he's searching for some way out of this.

'Maybe it'll come back to you on the way to the lake.' I gesture to the right with my gun. 'Off you go then – that way.'

He turns his head to look where I'm pointing. 'And how do you think that's going to work?' he says, looking down at the duct tape around his ankles.

He's right – he won't get very far with his feet strapped together. I didn't think of that. Silently I remove the tape. It's tricky with just one hand, but I don't want to put the gun down.

As I stand up again, he whirls around. I see the kick coming, but don't manage to get out of the way in time and his foot catches me in the stomach. The impact drives the air from my lungs and I topple backwards in agony. Gasping for air, I try to get back to my feet, my fingers still clamped around the pistol. He's already next to me, the light from his headtorch dazzlingly bright. Instinctively I roll to the side. His foot swings into thin air and he loses his balance. Scrambling to my feet, I jam the muzzle of the gun against his forehead.

'Try that again,' I warn him between large gulps of air, 'and you're dead.'

'You wouldn't shoot me,' he says, panting.

'I wouldn't count on it if I were you.' I press the gun harder against his head. We stare at each other. I have to force myself not to look away. He mustn't think I'm afraid of him.

The noise of a rapidly approaching vehicle breaks the silence, sending a flood of adrenaline coursing through my body.

'Move it!' I order him. 'You first.'

He doesn't budge – just stares back at me, defiance written across his face.

'If that car stops, I'm going to shoot the people in it and then I'm going to shoot you,' I say through gritted teeth.

David's expression remains unchanged.

The headlights reach the bare hedge that separates the car park from the road. I hold my breath. David's tension is almost as palpable as my own fear.

Don't stop. Please don't stop.

The car zooms past the turning.

'Must be your lucky day,' I say in relief, savouring David's evident disappointment.

He snorts.

'Shall we get going then?' I ask in a deliberately amiable tone.

David shoots me a venomous look and strides off. I hurry after him.

'I'm right behind you, remember,' I tell him. 'Try to run and I'll shoot. And believe me, that's no empty threat.'

We trudge in silence along the rain-sodden path, our headtorches cutting a narrow swathe of light through the darkness. There's an overpowering smell of damp earth. The ground is covered with mouldering leaf litter and so slippery that I nearly lose my footing a few times. The sky overhead is an impenetrable black, heightening the impression that we're making our way through a claustrophobic tunnel.

My phone rings again. I fish it out of my pocket to switch it off, but it slips through my fingers and lands in the wet leaves on the ground. Instinctively I bend down to retrieve it. There's a flash of movement in the corner of my eye and I look up. David has broken into a run.

11

I fumble for my phone, glimpsing Alexander's name on the display as I stuff it in my coat pocket despite the wet mud all over it, then I take off after David. Where's he gone? I caught a flash from his headtorch just now but it's been swallowed again by the darkness. I run on, my gun at the ready.

The path grows wider and starts to curve. Suddenly the clouds part and cold moonlight pours down over the lake, which emerges before me as if out of nowhere. Its surface is smooth and black, like a cloth spread taut over an unfathomable abyss. I stop in my tracks. It costs me some effort to tear my eyes away from the lake to look for David. He's down at the shoreline, hunched forwards and staggering like he's drunk. I break into a run. He hears me coming, glances over his shoulder and hurries onwards. I'm gaining on him; I'm already so close I can hear his ragged breath.

'Stop or I'll shoot,' I yell.

David comes to an immediate halt.

I raise the pistol, but then stumble and land flat on my face. Dazed, I lift my head.

David is coming straight for me.

I try to get up, but a shooting pain in my knee forces me back down. Where's my gun? It must have slipped from my fingers when I fell. My eyes flit back and forth under the light from my headtorch. There, right in front of me. I reach for it, but look up when I hear a sound. David. Quick as a flash, I snatch back my hand and his boot narrowly misses my fingers. He emits a howl of fury. I roll on my back but he's here, looming over me. Then I kick him in the crotch as hard as I can. He yelps and totters backwards, falls to his knees.

Despite the pain, I heave myself upright and grab the gun. David is still kneeling on the sand, gasping for air. I hobble towards him.

'Get up.'

He tries to stand, grimacing with the effort, and I watch his exertions coldly. I like seeing him so helpless. To my surprise, I realise I'm actually enjoying this.

'Look around you,' I say, once he finally staggers to his feet. 'Take in every detail.'

David pivots his head back and forth. The light from his head-torch sweeps over the darkness like a searchlight.

'Familiar in any way?'

He shakes his head, but his eyes give him away. He's lying.

'You've never been here before?' I ask him.

'No, for Christ's sake,' he wheezes.

He's a good actor, I have to give him that. But he can't fool me.

'OK, if that's how you want to play it,' I say. Then I gesture with the gun for him to head into the woods to our right.

There's no path, so we have to fight our way through the under-growth. David is clearly having trouble keeping his balance; he keeps stumbling, so it's slow going. The moon has crept behind a cloud and our headtorches bore tunnels of light into the darkness. I'm constantly looking over my shoulder as I can't shake the feeling that someone's following us, but I expect I'm just suffering from paranoia on top of everything else.

'Stop,' I say once we arrive at a small clearing. I'm not sure we're in the right place, but it doesn't really matter. 'Don't move.'

I put my backpack on the ground and take out the ankle cuffs.

'Stand by that tree with your back to me.'

'What are you going to do?' There's a distinct note of panic now in David's voice.

'Do you really have to ask?' I say. 'This has to remind you of something surely?'

'No!' he yells.

Out of nowhere, David whirls around and flings himself at me. I dodge to one side and he lands flat on the ground beside me. His face slams into the forest floor with a hideous crack.

I wasn't expecting him to attack me again. It takes me a second to recover from the shock. David doesn't move. I nudge him in the ribs with my toe. 'Come on. Get up.'

No response. He just lies there like a corpse. Is this a ruse? This time I give him a proper kick. Nothing. I hesitate slightly, then put the gun away and squat down beside him. Shoving both my hands under his torso, I try to roll him on to his back. He's heavier than he looks though; it takes a few goes to get him over. His headtorch glows up at me like a third eye. It survived the fall with surprisingly little damage. David's eyes are closed and blood is pouring from his nose. I lean down and listen to his breathing. Shallow but steady. He groans quietly and his eyelids start fluttering. He's coming round.

'What . . . ? How . . . ?' He stares woozily up at me.

'Welcome back to your own personal nightmare,' I reply.

'My nose,' he whimpers. 'What's wrong with my nose?'

He raises himself up, groaning all the while, only to fall back down. Then he immediately tries it again. The third time round, he manages to sit up with his legs splayed out in front of him. He looks dreadful – his face covered in blood, his nose swollen into a shapeless, cherry-red lump, his hair plastered to his forehead.

'I can't go any further,' he whimpers, his breath ragged.

'Bend your legs and brace your feet against the ground.' I grab his armpits from behind and push my weight against his back. 'Now.' With all my might, I heave David to his feet.

'Go and stand by that tree with your face against the trunk.'

He follows my instructions, his shoulders slumped.

'Can you still not remember?'

'No. I have no idea what you want from me.' His voice is so faint, it's barely audible. I can hear him sobbing.

Does he really think he can move me with his tears? He should know better by now. I attach the cuffs to his ankles and they lock into place with a quiet click. He lets it happen without any resistance. All the fight seems to have gone out of him.

'Turn around.'

I watch him shuffle about until we're standing face to face.

Somewhere close by, I hear the husky call of an owl. A strong wind has sprung up and is shaking the branches of the trees, but I'm pumped so full of adrenaline that I can't feel the cold. Quite the opposite, in fact: my insides are blazing with heat.

'You're insane,' David croaks.

'You may be right there, David darling.' I take out the roll of duct tape.

His eyes widen and he stares at me like I'm a visitor from another world. It's probably only just dawned on him what I have in mind.

'Help!' he screams. 'Help me!'

'Save your breath,' I tell him. 'No one can hear you.'

'What do you want me to say?' David asks pleadingly.

I shake my head. 'That's not how this works, my friend.'

His ribcage is working in and out, double time. He's scared to death; I can smell it from every pore of his body.

'Maybe I've been here before and forgotten.' He spits out the words as if each one is a struggle.

'Forgotten?' I reply scornfully.

'Yes, forgotten,' he gasps.

'Well then, try to remember.'

A tortured expression appears on his battered face. 'OK, yes, I've been here before.'

'And?'

'I did it,' he quickly replies.

'Did what?'

A hint of slyness creeps into his expression. His eyes narrow to slits. 'You do know a forced confession won't do you any good, right? The police won't—'

'I don't care about the police,' I cut in. 'You're going to die here. Whether you confess or not.'

2003

I'd recently passed my driving test and persuaded Mum to lend me her car. Now I was racing down the country road with the windows wound down and my hair streaming in the wind, breathing in the dust that wafted into the car from the parched fields, and singing loudly and a little off-key to the song I'd been listening to on repeat over the last few days: 'Spending My Time' by Roxette. I'd found the CD in my mother's collection while hunting for a suitable soundtrack to my heartbreak. The lyrics summed up my wounded feelings to a T.

I knew that Paul and the others had set off by bike on an expedition to some lake in Brandenburg and I couldn't bear the thought that he might have taken them to *our* lake. But I had to know. It was almost a compulsion.

Having worked myself up into tears by this stage, I arrived in the car park where Paul and I had set off for the lake together for the first and only time. If I threatened to kill myself, would he finally understand that no other woman would ever love him like I did? Would he acknowledge his own feelings for me at long last? I slung my bag over my shoulder and got out of the car.

With Paul's tender words 'I love you, Michaela' whispering in my ear, I headed down the narrow path. I was at war with myself the whole way – my rational mind telling me to turn back, but my emotions resisting with all their might. Paul was moving on. To Paris. It felt like the end of the world to me. I might never see him again. The very idea broke my heart.

Paul doesn't love you. When are you going to realise that? Just turn back. Those three sentences played continuously in my mind. By now I was sobbing and yet still I kept going. I loved Paul, but I hated him for what my love was making me do.

I could hear their carefree laughter off in the distance, and as I approached, I thought I could make out Paul's voice. Did he just say my name?

They're laughing at you, a voice whispered at the back of my mind. *They're making fun of your naivety. Your stupidity.*

A pang of sorrow hit me in the gut like a sledgehammer. Right this minute he could be telling the others every last detail of what we'd done together by the side of the lake. He might say that I'd called him multiple times a day ever since, leaving anguished messages declaring my undying love. That would be a betrayal beyond any hope of forgiveness.

The sun was hanging low in the sky, bathing the forest in a soft golden light, and a gust of wind ran through the treetops and ruffled the surface of the lake. Yet I barely registered the idyllic surroundings. I stopped, shading my eyes with my hand. Where were they? I'd heard their voices just now – or had I imagined it?

Their bikes were leant up against a couple of trees, apart from one that lay on the ground as if it had been dropped there. There was no sign of Paul and the others. The back of my neck started to prickle. Something didn't feel right.

I spotted the tents off to one side, in the shade of a couple of chestnut trees. Were the others inside maybe? I headed over and stumbled on a branch, but managed to catch myself just in time.

Hang on, what was that thing over there in front of me? A mass of golden fur, covered in fat, gleaming bluebottles. I gave a start. It was a dog. Corky? He was lying on his side with his legs splayed, a pool of blood oozing from his head. In a flash, I realised something terrible had happened. Every fibre of my being was screaming at me to get out of there as fast as I could, but I clamped down on the urge to run. What if Paul and the others needed me? Hesitantly, I pressed on.

A bare foot, its toenails jaunty with red nail varnish, was poking out of one of the tents. I reached out and started to push the door flap aside. Just then I heard a loud crack, of twigs snapping underfoot maybe, somewhere nearby. Startled, I leaped to my feet. Another crack. Someone was coming alright. I crouched behind the tent, my ears straining for the next sound, my heart pounding.

Silence.

It was probably just some old tree trunk creaking in the wind, I decided. I was about to stand up when I heard a rustling sound, like someone walking through dry grass. Quickly I hunkered down again and through sheer instinct held my breath. The footsteps drew closer and came to a stop in front of the tent. I held my hands over my mouth to muffle any sound that might give me away. For a while, all I could hear was the whisper of the wind in the trees. And then the silence was broken by a single piercing scream. My heart nearly stopped.

I could hear someone whispering. Was it a girl's voice? She was murmuring Paul's name over and over, followed by the names of the others.

It was Maike. Realising it was only her, I finally crept out of my hiding place. Maike was kneeling in front of the tent and rocking back and forth, her arms wrapped around her chest, although she leaped to her feet when she caught sight of me. Her cheeks were streaming with tears, horror etched on her face, as if it weren't me standing before her, but the devil himself.

I reached out a hand and said, 'It's only me, Maike. There's no need to be afraid.'

But I couldn't seem to get through to her. She shrank back, her eyes flitting from side to side as if she was looking for some way to escape. All of a sudden, she let out another shrill scream and dashed off. I was about to go after her when I spotted two figures down by the shore of the lake. Who could they be? Paul and Erik? But why on earth would Maike run away from them? Taking a closer look, I realised that I didn't know either of these guys. They broke into a run and followed Maike into the woods, and it seemed obvious their intentions weren't good.

Get out of here! cried my rational mind. *Find somewhere safe.* I hung back for a moment, but then ran after the others. I was so scared I felt sick, but I couldn't leave Maike on her own like that.

I had just caught sight of the two strangers when they came to a sudden stop. Hurriedly I ducked behind a tree, before peeking out a few seconds later. They hadn't budged and were talking in whispers. I could hardly believe my eyes. They were just teenagers. Two boys – both younger than me. One of them was tall and skinny with a face covered in acne, while the other was shorter and more stocky. But where was Maike? I couldn't see her anywhere. Had she managed to get away after all?

Just then, the taller of the two cupped his hands over his mouth and called out, 'Maike darling! Maike darling, where are you?'

The sound of his voice made all the hairs on my arms stand on end. Its softness was completely at odds with the threatening atmosphere and made my inner alarm bells scream all the more.

That was when I spotted Maike, crouching a few yards away from my own hiding place. I desperately wanted to help her but even though I had my father's revolver with me, I was too terrified to think straight – especially as it looked like the boys were armed.

The tall one was carrying a baseball bat and the shorter one had what looked like a gun.

The two boys started sauntering in her direction. They must have spotted her before I did and called her name to lull her into a false sense of security.

'Ah, there you are!' said the shorter of the two. He sounded almost glad to have finally found her.

They were playing a game with her – one that Maike was bound to lose. My pulse was racing. I was suddenly overwhelmed with fear that they might see me too and pulled myself back behind the trunk of my tree. *Why didn't you run away just now and get to safety?* A few short hours ago, I'd been picturing taking my own life, imagining how Paul would grieve over my tragic death. Now there was nothing I wanted more than to make it out of here in one piece. I threw my head back and stared up at the sky – as if I could expect any help from that quarter. The heavens were turning dusky grey. It would be dark before long. I started to properly panic.

Maike's voice carried over to me. It was little more than a pitiful squeak. The boy with the soft voice said something in return, but I couldn't make out what he was saying over the blood pounding in my ears. *Do something*, urged a whisper at the back of my mind. *You need to do something.* But I was paralysed with fear.

'Help me!' Maike shrieked all of a sudden. Her calls for aid echoed repeatedly through the woods – but no one came.

I burst into tears, slamming a hand over my mouth to muffle my sobs. I just wanted this nightmare to end.

My ears pricked up at some noises I couldn't identify, and then silence fell: a deathly silence, as if the whole forest and all its inhabitants were holding their breath.

What was happening? I couldn't stand the uncertainty any longer. Cautiously I shifted my weight. A loud crack beneath my feet broke the silence and I froze, listening hard. Had they heard me? I expected them to appear beside me at any second and drag me out from behind the tree, but nothing happened. With my body held tight against the trunk, I craned my neck and peered out.

Maike was lying face down, not moving, with her tormentors standing on either side of her. The taller of the two bent down and yanked her head up from the ground by her hair. Maike screamed, flailing wildly. Then the other boy's fist hit her square in the face. Even from my hiding place, I could hear the crunch of her nose. Her body went limp. With mounting horror, I watched the two of them drag their defenceless victim to the nearest tree, where they strapped her to the trunk and stuffed a gag into her mouth.

Soon after that, Maike came round. She started to whimper, jerking her head from side to side.

'You're in luck,' said the shorter one, standing directly in front of her and peering into her face. 'Isn't she, Leander?'

'Very much so, Felix,' replied the other one in his voice as soft as butter, as he moved next to his friend. 'We're going to let you live.'

'Take care now, Maike,' said the short one. Then they turned to leave, grinning from ear to ear.

I was about to pull back behind my tree when I saw Leander nudge his friend with his elbow and nod in my direction. Adrenaline surged through my body. They'd seen me. I broke cover and glanced over at Maike.

Don't leave me, she seemed to implore me with her eyes. *Help me. Please!*

But Leander was already moving towards me. Without a moment's hesitation, I spun on my heel and ran for my life.

12

David gives a sharp gasp. His eyes widen. 'Are you really going to kill me?' He can't quite hide the tremor in his voice.

'If I have to, yes. Though that would be far too lenient a punishment for your crime, if you ask me.'

'What have I ever done to you?'

'Nothing,' I reply, 'apart from destroying my life.'

'You've got the wrong person, I'm telling you.'

'You sound like a broken record,' I reply.

'I don't believe you,' he says, panting for breath. 'You couldn't kill anyone.'

'Are you sure about that?'

To my amazement, I find myself enjoying the situation more and more. I'm relishing the power I have over him. My nerves have vanished, giving way to a warm glow of calm authority. He can't hurt me anymore. I'm the one holding all the cards here. I want him to go insane with fear, to beg me for mercy. I want him to know what mortal terror feels like.

'Go on then – do it. Shoot me!' He sticks his chin out and fixes me with a look of pure defiance. 'Let's get this madness over with.'

'As you wish.'

Without taking my eyes off him, I back off to a spot a few yards away and grip my gun with both hands. Then I squint, take aim and fire.

David's knees give way. His scream is drowned out by the bang from the gun, which reverberates like a thunderclap through the forest. The silence afterwards is deep and heavy, as if the world stopped turning for a fraction of a second. A shudder runs up my back. Was that me just now? Did I really just fire a gun at another human being? I swallow.

'The next one won't miss,' I say hoarsely, before clearing my throat to get rid of the lump there. 'I guarantee you that.'

David makes a noise like the whine of a wounded animal and tries to stand upright, but he can't do it. I walk over to him, grab his arm and help him up. Only then do I notice the wet patch on his trousers. A faint smell of urine rises to my nostrils. He avoids catching my eye.

After that, he finally lets me strap him to the tree trunk in silence. I take off his headtorch. The bullet has torn a gash in David's cheek; his face is caked in dirt and blood. He seems paralysed, his body limp, as if the duct tape wrapped around his thighs is the only thing keeping him from falling. No pity now. It's only what he deserves.

'You're in luck,' I say, and pause for effect. 'Very much so.'

He jerks his head up and stares at me through bloodshot eyes, his expression hovering somewhere between hope and confusion. Maybe he's already guessed what I'm about to say.

'I'm going to let you live, David.'

He screams, but I reach him in two quick steps and stuff the gag in his mouth. David retches; his jaw starts to work frantically. His Adam's apple bobs rapidly up and down as I seal his lips with duct tape. He sucks in air through his nose and expels it again with a whistle on each breath.

'So, how does it feel?' I ask him.

His eyes beg me for mercy.

'Oh yes, that's exactly what I'm going to do,' I say in answer to his unspoken question. 'I'm going to leave you to your fate. Maybe you'll be lucky and someone will find you in time. But if I were you' – I purse my lips and shake my head with feigned regret – 'I wouldn't bank on it. Hardly anyone comes this way at this time of year. Just the odd wolf.'

I can't quite suppress my gloating as I peer into his bewildered face. David yanks desperately at his bonds, emitting pathetic squeals all the while. My nostrils are invaded by the acrid scent of his sweat – I can smell his sheer terror.

I catch myself feeling a tinge of compassion, but clamp down hard on it. If anyone deserves to suffer, it's David. He's not worth my pity.

2003

To this day, I don't know how I managed to escape from those boys. Fear lent me a strength I didn't know I had. I ignored the path, rushing headlong through the woods. Branches thwacked me hard in the face and thorns scratched my bare legs to ribbons. Hot blood ran down my skin. As if controlled by some external force, I leaped over tree trunks, pushed my way through the undergrowth with my bare hands, fell down, scrambled to my feet, and somehow found myself back in the car park, where I stared at my car for a few seconds in sheer disbelief. It seemed like a miracle. I broke down in tears, until a loud crack from the woods – or was it a bang? – jolted me back into action. I thought I could hear Leander's soft voice. With trembling hands, I fished the car key out of my bag and unlocked the door, then got in, tossing my bag in ahead of me. It landed on the edge of the passenger seat and half its contents spilled out, but I barely noticed as I started the ignition, shaking violently from head to toe, and gripping the steering wheel for support.

Only when I turned on to the main road to Berlin did I manage to collect my thoughts a little. I needed to call the police and summon an ambulance. Maike had still been alive when I left, though I didn't know how Paul, Juli and Erik were doing. I hadn't been able to look inside the tent and I feared the worst.

With one hand on the wheel, I pulled my bag towards me by the strap, unzipped the inner compartment and hooked out my phone – but it slipped through my sweaty fingers and fell on the floor. Cursing quietly, I slung the bag back on to the passenger seat and took my foot off the accelerator slightly. Steering with my left hand, I groped blindly around the footwell. No joy. The road ahead of me lay empty, so I glanced down at the floor. Luckily I spotted my phone straight away – it had slid partway under the seat. I reached down to grab it and sat back up only to find the road now bathed in glaring light. Dazzled, I squeezed my eyes shut for a moment. When I opened them again, a pair of headlights was hurtling straight towards me. Instinctively I flung the steering wheel to the left and slammed my foot on the brake. The car shot off the road and plunged into the undergrowth. I caught a brief glimpse of a tree trunk right in front of me and immediately afterwards felt the horrible impact – a metallic crunch. The bonnet crumpled like cardboard and the windscreen shattered. Electric pain shot through my body and the last thing I heard was a steady throbbing pulse. Then everything went black.

When I came to, there was a warm hand gently gripping my own. *Paul*, I thought. *Paul is here.* A feeling of joy surged through me. *Everything is OK.*

I opened my eyes, and as if that one small action had opened a floodgate, an unbearable tide of fiery agony coursed through my innards. I groaned. My surroundings were blurred. I blinked, attempting to focus, and little by little, the contours of the space around me took shape. Slowly I began to realise where I was. In hospital.

An IV bag dangled limply above me. Mum was sitting on a chair by my bed. It was her fingers, not Paul's, that lay cupping my hand. The disappointment cut my heart like a knife. She smiled at me and her lips moved, but no words came through. I raised my head and opened my mouth to speak, but could produce only incomprehensible sounds. I sank weakly back on to the pillow.

'Shhhh,' said Mum, leaning over me. She laid a gentle finger on my lips. 'It's all OK. Get some rest. You need to get better.'

I knew there was something important to tell her, but couldn't quite recall what it was. Every time I tried, my thoughts scattered before I could make sense of them. Exhaustion finally got the better of me and pulled me into a deep sleep, from which I kept jerking awake, drenched in sweat, with that soft voice echoing in my ears that had called out to Maike and left me in mortal terror.

It was another three days before I could put two sentences together and answer people's questions. Yet there were still large gaps in my memory, which the doctors put down to my accident. All I could remember was that something dreadful had happened by the lake. The hospital notified the police immediately.

Unfortunately, the whole region had been lashed by torrential rain the night after my escape, so all the evidence had been washed away. I only found out about that much later. Mum also held back the news about my friends for the first few days. The doctors had advised her not to say anything out of concern that I wouldn't cope with the awful truth. Maike had survived for three nights before choking on her own vomit. She'd died not long before they found her. Erik might have been saved if they'd got to him one day sooner, but Paul and Juli had obviously been dead for some time.

Nobody openly accused me of anything, but I couldn't shake the feeling that everyone secretly blamed me for their deaths.

I'd sustained serious injuries in the accident and had to spend several weeks in hospital before I was finally allowed home.

Physically I recovered well enough, and I was lucky to suffer no lasting damage beyond a few scars. But the fear lingered on. And it grew with every piece of the puzzle I retrieved from the depths of my memory, as little by little I reconstructed the sequence of those terrible events by the lake.

13

'Take care now,' I say.

Pure horror leaps out at me from David's eyes. He makes muffled noises, jerking his upper body back and forth. He looks pathetic. There's no trace left of his arrogant posturing.

I walk away with deliberate slowness, David's eyes burning into my back, but I don't turn round. As soon as I'm out of view, however, I can't help but pick up my pace. It's like I want to put as much distance between myself and my victim as possible. But I don't get very far. I'm completely spent, as if I've used up every last ounce of energy. My exhaustion mounts with every step I take, my legs so heavy that I'm barely able to set one foot in front of the other. My knees are weak and soon give way altogether, so that I drop like a boxer in the ring after the final knock-out.

What in God's name am I even doing here? It feels like I've spent the last few hours in some kind of trance. Did I really kidnap Toni's husband? To think that I shot at him too! The bullet could have killed him. What on earth has got into me? I must be completely out of my mind.

The wet soil I'm kneeling on has soaked my trousers, which are now clinging unpleasantly to my calves. Cold creeps through my body. With considerable effort, I haul myself to my feet. The gun in my hand suddenly feels alien. If I leave David back there he'll die, and then I'll be a murderer – no better than him. Whatever he did, however awful his crime, I have no right to put him to death.

Before I can stop myself, I raise my arm and ram the barrel of my gun against my temple so hard that I cry out. I could put an end to the whole thing right here and now. Free myself from the excruciating burden of guilt I bear for the deaths of my friends, who I let down when they needed me most. I wouldn't have to care then whether David dies or is rescued.

But I pause. My mother's face floats up in my mind's eye, with tears pouring down her cheeks. She would never understand why I'd killed myself; she'd spend the rest of her life blaming herself for not being able to stop me.

Slowly I lower the gun.

For a while I just stand there, arms dangling, head lowered. Then I turn round and trudge back.

David's outline appears before me in the cold LED glow of my headtorch. As I approach, he lifts his head and blinks at me, a mixture of fear and relief on his blood-smeared face. I come to a stop an arm's length from him. Silence. Not the slightest hint of a breeze. Not even a rustle from the undergrowth.

'I've given it some thought,' I say.

A flare of hope appears in David's eyes, which practically bore into my own.

'You have one small chance to save yourself,' I go on, trying to make my voice sound cold and hard.

His face twitches. He knows exactly what I want him to say.

'The summer of 2003,' I prompt him again. I don't add anything more. The rest needs to come from him.

He sucks in air through his nose, expels it again with a pained expression, and finally gives several nods.

'Good,' I say. 'I'm going to remove your gag.'

I step towards him and rip the duct tape from over his mouth.

He groans and works his jaw to spit out the handkerchief. I don't lift a finger to help him. The very idea of touching that damp rag disgusts me. Eventually he manages it without my help and spits the wet cloth out at my feet.

'I'm waiting,' I tell him.

'What guarantee do I have that you'll really let me go?' he croaks, licking his cracked lips.

'None at all. You'll just have to trust me.'

'Trust you?'

'Do you have a choice?'

'It was me,' he says.

'And? I want to know what you did.'

'I . . . raped you?' It sounds like a question. I think I can detect an almost gleeful note in his voice and anger boils up inside me.

'Are you making fun of me?' I cock the pistol and point it at him. 'Try that again and I'll pull the trigger.'

'OK, OK,' he says placatingly. 'What do you want to hear from me?'

'Details. Names. You can't have forgotten those.'

'Names,' he says, drawing the word out as if thinking carefully. 'Leander.'

'Yes,' I say. My pulse quickens. 'And?'

'That's the name of my baby son. Do you really want to rob him of his father? And Antonia of her husband? She's your friend.'

'Yes, Toni is my friend. That's exactly why I need to protect her from you.'

Suddenly David gives a start. His eyes are fixed on something behind me. I cast a glance over my shoulder.

A figure emerges from between the trees and heads straight for us. Who on earth could it be? Shock runs through me like a white-hot laser.

14

Blinding light. I instinctively shut my eyes and turn my face. David makes a strangled sound and continues to stare over my shoulder. His lips form three almost soundless words, but I understand them all the same. He says, 'Oh God, Erik.'

It takes me a few seconds to recognise the man hurrying towards us.

Alexander.

David has clearly mistaken him for Erik.

Alexander stops in front of us and I quickly hide the gun behind my back. His eyes flit briefly to David, then back to me.

'What on earth were you thinking?' His voice has a sharp, icy undertone.

'I . . . Well . . .' I splutter, before ducking behind a counter-question. 'How did you know I was here?'

'I was with your mother in the bookshop. She'd just discovered your online order. Chloroform and tasers aren't things people buy every day. She's beside herself with worry.'

I'm struck by the hot, sickening realisation that I forgot to clear the search history. I'd looked up the co-ordinates of the lake on the bookshop computer too, so it wouldn't have been hard to track me down.

Alexander shoves me aside and takes several strides towards David.

'Wait,' I say, grabbing his arm. 'Please.'

'Stop it, Michaela,' he snaps, shaking my hand off.

'When he saw you just now,' I say, lowering my voice, 'he whispered Erik's name.'

'Why would he . . . ?' Alexander looks baffled, but then lowers his voice too. 'You mean, he thought I was Erik?'

'Exactly,' I say with an emphatic nod, although I'm no longer entirely sure I didn't mishear him. Did he really say, 'Oh God, Erik'? Or did it just sound like it?

'You've got to help me,' David gasps. 'This madwoman' – he nods at me – 'has kidnapped and tortured me. She's spent the whole time yammering on at me about how I need to confess something, but I have no idea what she wants from me. I haven't done anything to her.'

'Don't be afraid. I'm a police officer,' Alexander reassures him. 'I'm going to untie you and then we'll all drive back to the station in Berlin and sort everything out.'

David just flinched at the words 'police officer' – I'm sure I didn't imagine that. I frantically try to figure out what I can do to turn the tide back in my favour.

'Please don't,' I beg Alexander. 'I've nearly worn him down. He's about to confess.'

'No,' says Alexander firmly. 'This stops here. You've already done enough damage.'

'But I'm absolutely certain David is one of the murderers from back then.'

'Just like all the other times?'

I stare at him, my eyes bulging. 'How do you know about that?'

'I read it in the addendum to the case file.'

'The case file?' I echo, confused.

'Yes. I asked for a copy a few days ago to take home with me and review in my spare time.'

'But . . .' I hesitate. 'Why?'

'The case is going to be reopened at my request,' he says. 'I've come across a few inconsistencies and . . .' Alexander breaks off. He's spotted the gun in my hand. 'Give it to me.'

Shaking my head, I shrink back a step. I can see Alexander's mind whirring. Is he wondering whether to take it from me by force?

'It's fake,' I say quickly, glancing across at David – but he doesn't seem to have heard my lie.

'OK,' says Alexander cautiously. 'All the same, I'd prefer you to put it away.'

I stuff the gun into my backpack, but leave the bag unzipped so I can grab it again if I need to. David can't be trusted.

Alexander starts removing the duct tape while David glances between me and his rescuer. There's an unsettling glint in his eye, and my unease grows when Alexander peels off the tape from David's wrists too.

'Shouldn't you at least leave his hands tied?' I ask.

'There's absolutely no reason to,' Alexander says in a frosty tone. 'The guy's on the verge of collapse, can't you see? Now give me the key to his ankle cuffs.'

I hesitate. Alexander raises his eyebrows and holds his hand out expectantly. Right this minute, he seems like my enemy. As if he's joined forces with David against me.

'What's taking so long?' he says insistently.

I reach inside my coat and hand him the key, but I don't feel good about it. Alexander's making a big mistake and I can't do a thing to stop him.

David groans, rubbing his wrists and rolling his shoulders, while Alexander unlocks the ankle cuffs.

Hang on – what was that? I peer into the forest. Did something just bark? There it is again! It almost sounds like a muffled cough. Is there someone else sneaking around out there? Did Alexander tell his colleagues before setting off to find me? I've barely finished my thought when a gunshot shatters the silence.

I scream in terror and wheel round. Alexander is lying on the ground, with David leaning over him and looking down at his body. The bullet hit Alexander square in the face. There's blood pulsing from the wound. His body is twitching, with inarticulate noises coming from his mouth. His eyes search for mine – beg me to help him – but I'm paralysed with horror. David totters towards me, his eyes glittering with bloodlust. What's that in his hand? A pistol? He lifts his arm. I turn and flee, expecting at any second to feel a bullet slam into my back and send me flying. Without stopping to think, I follow the narrow strip of light from the beam of my torch in the darkness, one single word hammering away in my brain: *RUN!*

15

Wet branches hit me hard in the face. Thorns tear at my trousers. Pushing my way through the vegetation with my bare hands, I stumble over something, but catch my balance just in time and then hurry onwards, arms flailing. My eyes flit wildly back and forth as I try to find a way through the densely packed trees. David must be right behind. I cast a hasty glance over my shoulder. Why can't I see him? I fall, but scramble back to my feet. The stitch in my side comes out of nowhere; hunching over, I press my hand down over the sore spot and battle on through the undergrowth. Surely I'm going to come across a path at some point. The forest isn't that big. Another glance back. Still no David. Have I lost him? I manage to stagger on for a few more steps until the pain in my side forces me to halt. Bent over double, I pause to gather myself. My heart is beating fast and unevenly; my lungs are burning from the strain. The noisy rasp of my breath drowns out everything else around me. I need to keep going. I can't be sure that David isn't still following.

It's raining, I suddenly realise. I start moving again and pull my hood up. It looks like the forest is thinning out up ahead. I aim in that direction and, sure enough, I soon find myself in a small clearing with a wooden structure in the middle. The sodden ground squelches beneath my feet as I hurry towards the raised hunting hide. It looks in reasonable condition, as far as I can tell. If hunters are using it, there also has to be a trail to this point. I search in vain for footprints in the mud and eventually chance across a narrow path, praying that it'll lead me out of the woods.

The rain is getting heavier now; a gust of wind throws my hood back and I yank it over my head again. My face is stinging from the cold and my feet are aching. There's no way I can keep this up for much longer. It's already a battle just to put one foot in front of the other. The wind whistles more and more fiercely through the bare branches. A loud crack from somewhere close by gives me such a start that I scream. What was that? My heart thudding in my chest, I peer into the trees but can't make out anything that shouldn't be there in the faint glow of my headtorch. Probably just a branch snapping off in the storm. I need to find a way out of this forest as soon as I can, before I'm hit by a falling tree.

Wait – what's that up ahead? Panic robs me of my breath. Is it some sort of animal? I gasp for air. It looks like a dog. Does it belong to one of the hunters? Hope flares up inside me and I take a hesitant step towards the four-legged creature, which remains motionless in the beam of my torch. Then I take a closer look. Grey shaggy fur, pointed snout, lean body. Oh my god, that's no dog, I realise in a flash. It's a wolf! And the rest of the pack is probably lurking just out of sight. The creature bares its teeth. I swallow. Should I yell at it? Beat a hasty retreat? I instinctively opt for the latter and pray that I'm making the right choice. Without taking my eyes off the wolf for a second, I start to withdraw with slow, cautious steps.

Another loud crack – from above? Behind? Seconds later, a hard object hits me in the head with such force that I crumple to my knees. The world goes black and the ground gives way beneath me. My last thought is, *David*.

I wake up to a scritch-scratching right next to my ear. Where am I? What happened? Then it all comes rushing back. David knocked me out. Or was it just a falling branch? I sit up too fast and immediately feel dizzy and sick. A dull ache is thumping away in my skull. Delicately I probe the back of my head and wince when I find the wound. When I look down at my hand, my fingertips are red with blood. I wipe them on my trousers, struggle to my feet and look around.

The wolf is standing six feet away and staring at me with its bright eyes, as if trying to hypnotise me. My heart thunders in my chest. It's still here. Wolves are carnivores, of course. They kill sheep. But do they attack humans too? I wish I knew. Once again I back away, one careful step at a time. The creature follows my retreat with watchful eyes but doesn't move. Shuffling backwards, I bump into a tree and give a shout of surprise, nearly losing my balance. When I look back up, the wolf is gone.

I whirl around, anxious to avoid an attack from behind or from the side, but the forest is deserted. The wolf has vanished as if it was never there in the first place. I breathe a deep sigh of relief and walk on.

It's not long before I come across a path, and the hope of making it out of the forest gives me fresh energy. I march on and on but the path seems never-ending. Before long, each step is a struggle. The wound on the back of my head is throbbing, but I grit my teeth and drag myself painfully onwards. *Don't stop, whatever you do – or you'll never get moving again.*

A sound drifts towards me. A car engine? My heart gives a brief flutter. There must be a road nearby. At that very moment, the light of my headtorch flickers and goes out, leaving me in complete darkness.

'Come on, come on,' I murmur, frantically switching it off and on again. All around me is a gaping black void, full of strange creaks and rustles and the calls of unseen animals. Fear starts to creep up inside me as I continue desperately flicking the switch. On. Off. On. Off. At long last, the bulb comes back to life. I walk on more quickly now, praying for it not to go out again.

The path widens. Is that the road up ahead? My torch starts to flicker once more. *Faster – you need to move faster.* I hurry onwards, stumbling over my own feet a few times in sheer panic, but by now I can clearly make out the dark strip of the road. The relief is overwhelming and by the time I reach the edge of the woods, I'm laughing and sobbing all at once.

Instinctively I strike off to my right, praying for a car to come by and pick me up, in spite of the late hour.

All through my terror-fuelled escape, I haven't once stopped to think about what happened down by the lake – which means the memory hits me all the harder now. Alexander is dead. Murdered by David. A thick lump forms in my throat. Why did he do it? Did he honestly think it was Erik? Did Alexander have to die because David mistook him for the only person who could have identified him as the killer? The more I think about it, the more doubtful that seems. The crime was all over the news at the time, so David must know that Erik is dead. Maybe he heard Alexander talk about reopening the case. That might have scared him so much that he saw no other option than to kill him. And I was probably next on his list.

I have to tell the police, I realise suddenly. Before David makes his escape and once again avoids being held to account for his crimes. I reach into my coat. Where's my phone? I'm sure I put it in my pocket. I pat myself down, but it's not in the inner pockets either. I must have lost it while I was running through the woods. Could things get any worse? I want to cry.

Just then, the sound of another engine grabs my attention. Headlights slice through the black night and hurtle towards me so fast that I only manage to react when the car is within a few yards of me. I leap into the road, fling my arms over my head and wave frantically. Barely bothering to slow down, the car just weaves around me and races onwards. My arms drop to my sides and I stare after it in bewilderment. The rear lights glow like red-hot coals as the vehicle rounds the corner and vanishes into the darkness.

'Arsehole!' I roar at the top of my voice.

Who on earth would leave someone standing on a deserted road in the middle of the night? What kind of person does that? Anger lends me new strength and I trudge on bitterly.

16

I've been dragging myself along the narrow roadside verge for what feels like an eternity now. Every few yards, my headtorch flickers and throws me into complete panic, sending hot waves of adrenaline through my bloodstream. The moon has crept behind a thick layer of cloud and the whole world seems black as sin. I'm exhausted, beyond cold or pain, planting one foot in front of the other like a robot. The same sentence keeps running through my mind: *You need to keep moving.* Several cars have already sped past, but none slowed down, let alone stopped for me. It's like I'm invisible.

And now I hear the rumble of a new car approaching from behind, some time before its headlights cast their yellow glare on the roadway in front of me. I wait, hoping to catch the driver's attention, but I'm so weak by this time that I'm no longer capable of raising my arms. They dangle like useless dead weights at my side. Whatever. The car's not going to stop in any case.

Slowly I start off again, but then the discordant squeal of brakes cuts through the night. Right on cue, my torch flickers and goes out, but the car pulls over directly alongside me. The passenger window slides down and a figure leans over from the driver's side. I can just about see the outline of a face.

'Who on earth left you out here?' It's a woman's voice: deep, hoarse and slightly too loud.

She peers at me with bright, curious eyes that remind me oddly of the wolf from earlier. Her pale face is framed by thick black curls.

'I got lost,' I croak. 'Can you give me a lift?'

'To Berlin?'

I nod.

'Sure. Get in.' Without waiting for a reply, she winds the window back up.

Before I open the door, I take off my headtorch, waver for a moment and toss it into the grass. Then I flop into the seat and tuck my backpack into the footwell. The woman looks me up and down as I buckle my seatbelt. Only now do I realise how awful I must look – on my last legs, covered in filth, my hair sticky with blood.

'Hi, I'm Irena,' she says as she puts the car into gear, 'but everyone calls me Ira.'

'Michaela,' I reply. 'Thanks for the lift.'

'So who did that to you? Your fella?'

'No.' I shake my head. 'No, it wasn't like that.' I'm so tired, it's a struggle to get the words out.

'I see – you don't want to talk about it. That's OK. When I was your age, I'd be ashamed every time too when my man beat me. You get over it though. In the end I started hitting him back.' She gives a loud cackle, but it sounds forced.

I glance furtively across at her. Her eyes are surrounded by a fine mesh of countless wrinkles and her hair is threaded with streaks of grey. She's also dressed from head to toe in black. She's older than I initially thought – about my mother's age. I can detect a hint of alcohol on her breath, I think, but right now I couldn't care less. I'd get in a car with the devil himself if he promised to take me to Berlin.

Ira turns on the radio. 'Mind if we listen to some music?'

'Not at all.'

I lean back into the seat and close my eyes. Just a quick nap. As the gentle trumpets of an unfamiliar jazz band float into the car, I slowly drift off – only to shoot wide awake with a shriek when somebody grabs my arm. My first thought is, *David – he's found me!*

'Sorry, I didn't mean to scare you.'

I look around in confusion and realise I'm sitting in a moving car with an unfamiliar woman at the wheel.

'Did I fall asleep?'

'You were snoring like a freight train,' the driver chuckles.

Her name is Ira, I remember that now. I rub my hands over my face and yawn. When I look out of the window, I notice we're already in Berlin. Even though it's late, the pavements are packed with people walking briskly in thick coats and scarves. In front of us, a red-eyed snake of vehicles slithers towards the next set of traffic lights. I've never been so glad to get back to the bustling confusion of the capital.

'Where should I drop you?' Ira asks, her eyes glued to the road. 'Alexanderplatz?'

'Perfect,' I say.

There's a police station there. That'll be my first stop. Though I should have asked to borrow Ira's phone so I could call the police as soon as I got in the car. Why have I only thought of that now?

Over the dying notes of a tenor sax, the radio DJ announces that it's midnight and time for the news. I listen with half an ear, planning what I'm going to say to the police. I can't gloss over any of the details – I need them to trust me. After all, I already have a reputation as far as they're concerned. It's not going to be easy, but this time I saw the murder with my own eyes. I can testify with certainty that David killed someone. The thought of Alexander's horrible death unleashes a torrent of emotions in me: grief, anger and guilt. None of this would have happened if I hadn't kidnapped

David. What on earth possessed me? I look out of the window and blink away my tears.

'And finally, we have an important announcement from the police,' the newsreader declares in sonorous tones.

My ears prick up.

'Earlier this evening, a police officer was killed in a woodland area in the Schorfheide nature reserve. The prime suspect is a woman, who is armed and remains at large. We'll provide further updates as more information becomes available.'

I feel like I've been slapped in the face. How can the prime suspect be a woman? Then I go hot and cold in quick succession.

'What the hell?' Ira yells suddenly. She slams on the brake and leans on the horn. 'You're supposed to indicate when you change lanes! What do you think those little flashing lights are for, moron?'

David has turned the tables on me. The realisation hits me with such force, it leaves me breathless. I forgot to take his phone. He must have called the police from the scene of the crime. They're probably out looking for me already.

'Are you OK?' Ira asks, her voice filled with compassion.

To my surprise, I feel a sudden need to confide in her, but I suppress the urge. She's a total stranger. What grounds would she have to believe me?

'Yes, yes, I'm fine,' I reply.

She glances across at me. 'You sure?'

'I'm sure,' I say.

Through the windscreen, I see the Fernsehturm towering over Alexanderplatz. A mast covered in flashing red lights reaches up into the sky from the top of the revolving restaurant. In front of the tower, the facade of the Galeria Kaufhof department store glows in a vibrant green.

I suddenly feel like I'll suffocate unless I get some fresh air.

'You can drop me at the next set of lights,' I force myself to say. 'I'll walk the rest of the way.'

'As you wish,' Ira says slowly.

I'm on the verge of tears.

'Here, take my business card.' She passes one over to me. I have no idea where she conjured that up from.

Before I can reply, she says, 'Look, call me if you want. Any time, OK?'

'But you don't even know me,' I say in bemusement.

'You remind me of someone,' she says in her husky voice. 'A lot, actually. Someone who asked me for help, and who I let down when she needed me. I get the feeling you're in a similar situation.'

'Thank you.' I gulp down the lump in my throat and tuck the card in my pocket. 'And thanks again for the lift, Ira,' I add with a timid smile.

'Look after yourself, OK?' Ira stops at a red light. 'Off you go then,' she says. Her voice is determinedly cheerful, but I can hear the underlying sadness all too well.

'Bye then.' I grab my backpack from the footwell and scramble out.

Once I'm on the pavement, I turn to face her and raise my hand in farewell. She waves and drives off. A feeling of melancholy settles over me, and I almost regret getting out of the car. I feel defenceless and vulnerable – like I'm all alone in the world and there's absolutely no one I can turn to for help.

17

A woman hurrying past glances at me, wrinkles her nose and quickens her pace as if I'm infected with something. She must take me for a tramp – a down-and-out – though that's no reason to look at me like that. I feel like running after her and setting her straight on a few things about life, but I'm far too tired, so I just lower my head and trudge onwards.

It's only when I reach Alexanderplatz that I realise there's no point in going to the police. They'll just arrest me on the spot on suspicion of murdering Alexander. I should go home, get some rest, recover my strength and weigh up my options. I cross the concourse of the U-Bahn station and drag myself up the steps to the platform. When I'm nearly at the top, I suddenly realise my apartment is a no-go too. The police might be searching it right now, in which case I'd fall straight into their hands. I stop in my tracks. A train pulls in, drawing to a halt with a squeal. The doors open and a handful of people bustle past me down the stairs.

Where else can I go? To my mum's? The police will have been there too by now. She'll be distraught, poor thing – beside herself with worry. Instinctively I reach into my pocket, but then remember I've lost my damn phone. I turn and trudge back down the steps, sheer exhaustion nearly bringing me to my knees. Above all, I'm longing for a hot bath and a comfy bed.

There's something eerie about the garish neon lighting in the entrance hall to the station. I wander the corridors in search of a working payphone. Eventually I track one down near the left-luggage lockers. Mum picks up on the first ring, as if she was expecting my call.

'Hello?' she says, an anxious tremor in her voice.

'It's me,' I reply, and promptly burst into tears.

'Darling, where are you? Why didn't you answer my calls? I thought you were with Alexander! The police were here – they found your car. They told me you killed a man?' Her voice gets more and more shrill with every sentence.

'It wasn't me,' I sob. 'It was David.'

'David?' she replies, sounding nonplussed. 'Who's David?'

'Toni's husband.'

'What—?'

'It's too complicated to explain over the phone, Mum. It's . . .' By now, I'm crying so hard I can't get the words out.

Out of the corner of my eye, I see two police officers sauntering over in my direction. I quickly look away and murmur into the receiver, 'I'll call you back.' Then I hang up and wipe the tears from my cheeks.

I'll have to go past them to get to the exit. Pulling my hood down low over my face, I set off towards them with my shoulders hunched and my eyes glued to the floor. I'm so jumpy, I could throw up. The two officers – a man and a woman – are so wrapped up in their conversation that they barely seem to register my presence.

Stay calm – you're almost there.

I hold my breath and walk past. Only a few more yards and I'll be out and away.

'Hey, you!' a male voice calls after me. 'Wait a second!'

I pretend not to hear and force myself to keep walking at a normal speed instead of breaking into a run. Footsteps approach rapidly from behind and my heart skips a beat. It's too late. They've got me. I stop and slowly turn round, ready to face my fate.

'Here you go!' The kindly policeman hands me my backpack. 'You left it by the phone over there.'

'Oh,' I say, taking it and forcing a smile. 'How stupid of me. Thank you so much.'

'No problem at all,' he replies. As he's talking, his eyes are scanning my face. I can feel myself turning red.

'Anything else we can do for you?' he enquires.

'No, no,' I reassure him. 'I fell over earlier, but apart from a few bumps and bruises, I'm fine.'

'I see,' he says, but I can tell he doesn't believe a word of it.

'Thanks again,' I say quickly. 'Bye then.'

I make a beeline for the exit, expecting him to call me back at any moment – but I make it out of the station without further incident.

18

I cross the tram tracks and walk past the brightly lit windows of the Galeria Kaufhof. The Christmas market lies abandoned under the glow of the streetlights – the stalls boarded up, the carousels still and silent. A solitary crow stands on the pavement pecking at some tasty little morsel.

I have absolutely no idea where to go next. My stride slows as I mull over the possibilities. I can't go to a hotel because they normally want to see your ID when you check in and it's just too risky.

A life-sized poster showing the author of a bestselling thriller grins at me from the foot of an advertising column. He's posing confidently, sitting on a stack of copies of his latest book and brandishing another in his hand.

Of course! The obvious solution is so often the last one you think of.

Even Oranienburger Strasse, its narrow pavements heaving with tourists by day, lies deserted at this hour. A tram rattles past. The lights are still on in a few of the bars, but most have already shut up shop, and there's not a soul around as I make my way to the bookshop.

A draught of warm air and the clean, familiar scent of crisp new paper waft into my face as I open the door. How I love that smell. Every time I come through that door, I savour it all over again, and this evening is no exception, in spite of the circumstances. Yet I can't quite locate my usual sense of comfort and safety here today. I feel like an intruder somehow. My hand reaches automatically for the light switch by the door, but I snatch it back at the last moment. Bad idea. I feel my way across the dark shop floor towards the kitchen, where I shut the door behind me and pull down the blinds before turning on the light. Then I hang my coat on the rack and pull my boots off my aching feet. I take a bottle of water from the cupboard next to the fridge and drain half of it in one go. After that, I start to feel a little better. I pad over to the kitchen table in my socks, sit down on one of the chairs and rest my head on my arms. What unspeakable predicament have I got myself into here? I feel like crying all over again, but I'm too depleted even for tears.

I could do with a few hours' sleep to clear my head. Bracing my hands against the tabletop, I rise stiffly to my feet. Before I leave the kitchen, I remember to drape my wet coat over the chair and leave it to dry in front of the radiator. Then I turn out the light and shuffle over to the sofa in the corner of the shop. The pale light of pre-dawn filters through the slats of the front window blinds, and there's a comforting gurgle from the heating system. I just about manage to pull the woollen throw over myself before falling fast asleep.

I wake with a jolt and sit up as if someone's jabbed me with a cattle prod. The throw slides to the floor. What was that? I peer frantically around the shop. The outlines of the bookshelves are visible in the grey morning light, but dark shadows still lurk in every corner. My pulse takes a while to settle. Every part of my body hurts and my mouth tastes revolting. A tram rumbles past outside; the city is slowly waking up to a brand new day. I haul myself to my feet with a groan, feeling groggy.

You need to get out of here before Mum shows up. The realisation hits me on my way to the kitchen – my first clear thought since waking up. Knowing her, she'd talk me into handing myself in to the police. I scribble her a quick note on the back of an order form.

Dear Mum,

Don't worry, everything will be OK. I'll call as soon as I can.

Love, Michaela

PS – I've lost my phone.

I leave the note in an obvious spot on the kitchen table and then squeeze myself in front of the sink in the tiny bathroom. My pallid face stares back at me from the mirror. A graze on my right cheek is crusted over with dried blood and I'm developing a fine black eye on one side. Probably from a branch hitting me in the face, I'm guessing. My hair is a complete mess and the cut on the back of my head is throbbing like hell. No wonder Ira thought I'd been beaten up when she first set eyes on me. I wash my face and dab carefully at the raw skin on my cheek until it's dry. It stings, but it's stopped bleeding now at least. I might as well not have bothered with combing my hair though – it looks even worse than before, I think to myself with a grim smile. I don't have a toothbrush or paste so I rinse my mouth as well as I can with water. My stomach informs me with a growl that I need something to eat, but the only thing in the fridge is a mouldy piece of cheese. That goes in the bin and I content myself with drinking the rest of the bottled water from earlier. Then I slip into my coat – which by now is warm and dry on the outside, but unpleasantly damp on the inside – pull on my backpack and step out on to the street.

The temperature must have dropped below freezing overnight. The roofs of the parked cars are covered in a thin layer of frost. Ice crystals glitter under the streetlights. The new day is still shrouded in dusky grey, but it won't be long now before the sun comes up and Hackescher Markt fills with people.

I rub my hands together and shiver, hunching my shoulders. Right now, there's nothing I'd like more than to flee back into the warm and familiar surroundings of the bookshop. Picking a direction at random, I strike off down Oranienburger Strasse towards Friedrichstrasse, meeting hardly anyone on the way. I'm faint with hunger by this time. Close to the train station, I come across a near-deserted café. I duck inside and order a croissant and a cup of coffee at the counter, but when I come to pay, I realise I'm nearly out of cash. That's all I need. I pick up my tray and huddle in a corner. Besides me, there's only one other customer – a young woman absorbed in her phone. I take a sip of my cappuccino and then bite into the croissant. It tastes of cardboard, but I devour it greedily all the same. Then I shove the tray across the table and lean back in my chair.

So what now? Somehow I need to prove it was David who shot Alexander, not me. What about Toni? No, I can forget her. She'd never say or do a thing that might hurt her precious David. Especially not now she's had the baby.

Lost in thought, I stare at the television flickering on the opposite wall. The café is starting to fill up, the background buzz getting louder. Time to go. I stand up, but freeze when I see my own face staring back at me from the screen of the TV. With a sudden feeling that every single person in the room is also staring at me, I dash out on to the street and into the road without stopping to check if anything's coming. Got to keep moving.

Under the railway bridge there's traffic, and I cross the road between two idling cars. The acrid stench of their exhaust fumes brings on a fresh wave of nausea. I run towards the station and don't stop until I get to the public toilets, where I stumble into a cubicle, my fist clenched against my stomach. I feel a little better once I've brought up my breakfast. My pulse gradually evens out too, but I can't shake that feeling of being watched from all sides. I'm probably just imagining it, but to be on the safe side, I pull my hood up and lower my head as I walk across the concourse.

I can't stop thinking about what Alexander said by the lake. He mentioned that my case was going to be reopened and that he was going through the file. That he'd noticed some inconsistencies. Did David hear that too? Is that why he murdered him?

I need to see that file. But how can I get hold of it? Wait – didn't he say he was going through it at home in his spare time? My heart gives a nervous flutter of excitement.

The train to Frohnau is already at the platform; the doors are beeping, ready to close, the lights above them flashing red. I just manage to squeeze myself into a packed carriage before the doors slam shut behind me.

19

Back at Toni's housewarming party, Alexander mentioned that he'd moved into the house where his late parents used to live. I've only been there once before, when Erik threw a huge birthday party. That was the night Paul bet his friends that he could get me into bed, which is why he came on to me. Though I didn't know all that back then, of course. I quickly push the thought out of my mind.

After a while, the train empties and I can finally take a seat by the window, where I stare broodingly out at the buildings as they rush past. If I could turn back the clock, would I do it again? Kidnap David, just to find out the truth? Probably not. But now that Alexander is dead, all because of me, I have no choice but to keep going. I think of Toni and her baby, of how painful it'll be for her when she finds out who her husband really is. Will she be strong enough to bear the knowledge that he's a murderer or will it break her?

I'm pulled out of my reverie when the next stop is announced as Frohnau. I get off the train and hurry up the steps towards the exit. Annoyingly, I can't bring to mind the name of the street where Alexander's parents lived, only that it's on a cul-de-sac close to a graveyard.

Frohnau might be part of Berlin, but it feels like a small town once you get away from the station. The streets are narrow and lined with trees and detached houses with manicured gardens. Shortly before I reach the graveyard, I come across a dead-end road off to my right. This has to be it. I follow the cobbled street up to the very last gate. The edge of the garden is set back a few yards from the road, and beyond it stands an old house hiding behind three huge trees as if it's ashamed of its dirty grey walls. I look to check there's no one around before pushing on the handle of the garden gate. It swings open with a loud squeal, as if in protest at my trespassing. There are obvious spots of mildew on the net curtains and the windows haven't been cleaned in an age. The front garden is nearly hidden under several piles of bricks.

The property looks abandoned, but I ring the bell all the same. Alexander might have had housemates. If somebody opens up, I'll just pretend I've got the wrong place. I ring twice, but no one comes to the door. There's a narrow path off to my right and I follow it round to the back garden, which is overgrown, as if no one has tended it in years. A wooden bench is leant up against the back wall of the house next to a green plastic water butt. To the right of that are the stairs to the cellar – worn concrete steps leading down to a narrow door painted with creosote. Locked, of course. I push my whole weight against it, but the door doesn't budge an inch.

I wander back up the steps and take a closer look at the windows. The wooden frames are badly in need of a fresh coat of paint and show clear signs of decay. Both rear windows are set at about head height. Suddenly I remember the stacks of construction material I saw in the front garden. I head back up the path and return clutching a heavy brick, then shunt the bench under the window and climb on to it. It creaks alarmingly under my weight and wobbles, but manages to hold together. Gripping the brick, I smash it into the window on a spot roughly level with the latch. The glass shatters into a crazed web of countless tiny cracks. I strike again and this time several shards fall out, leaving a hole big enough for me to stick my hand through. I drop the brick on to the lawn behind me, reach inside, minding the broken glass, and fiddle with the latch. The window pulls open.

By this time I'm drenched in sweat and there's blood dripping from my hand; I must have cut myself and not noticed. I snatch a tissue out of the packet in my coat and press it against the wound for a few seconds. Luckily it's not very deep, but it stings all the same. With my other hand, I pull the window open a little further, then drop my backpack on the bench and climb into the house.

Once inside, I turn to close the window and notice with absolute horror the apartment block opposite. It can't be more than a hundred feet away. Is that someone on the balcony looking down at me – up there, in the top-right corner? I squint and peer upwards, only to realise with relief that it's not a person, just a folded parasol. I'm left feeling jumpy all the same. What if one of the residents saw me break in just now and is already on the phone to the police? I need to be quick.

I've landed in the kitchen. There's a pile of dirty pans and crockery in the sink and a smell of frying in the air, as if Alexander had only just gone out. Trying not to think about him, I cross the room and end up in a narrow hallway with two doors. One leads through to a bedroom, which reeks of Alexander's aftershave, while the other opens into the living room. I spot a folder on the coffee table and pick it up. On the spine, in faded handwriting, I see the year 2003, and below that the words *Murder of Paul Wagner*, followed by the names of Erik, Juli and Maike. I open the folder, only to shut it again immediately when a photo of the crime scene leaps out. There's no need to put myself through that right now. I slap the folder back on the table, and that's when I see the pad of paper which Alexander was clearly using to take notes – except that I can barely make out his handwriting. The letters 'DNA' in capitals stand in the middle of the page with a circle around them and several arrows pointing away from them, but the rest of the scrawl is so untidy that I can't read it for the life of me. I turn to the next page, but it's blank. He doesn't seem to have got very far with his notes.

Just then, I hear the sound of a car approaching. I dash to the window, lift the net curtain a fraction and peer out.

20

The car pulls up right in front of the house. I jump back from the window. So I was right after all – my break-in didn't go unnoticed. I rip the top page from the notepad and stuff it in my pocket as I'm hurrying through to the kitchen. As I open the window, the squeak of the front door seems to resonate through the house like a warning. I hop on to the windowsill and lower myself down on to the bench, snatch up my backpack and rush headlong through the garden. The property is bordered by a picket fence, and behind that I can see a path winding its way through a small copse of birch trees.

I glance back over my shoulder. There's a man standing on the rickety bench, inspecting the broken window. From his height and his posture, he seems strangely familiar. Wait a second – isn't that . . . ? He turns round now to scan the garden. Oh my God, it's Robert! I dart behind a tree. What the hell is he doing here? A few seconds later, I peer out from my hiding place and watch as he takes the path back round to the front with his phone to his ear. Was that really him or is my overstimulated brain playing tricks on me? Either way, I need to get out of here.

I check my surroundings. Tucked behind a bush, I spot an array of soil-covered flowerpots, buckets and other garden tools. I pick up the largest bucket, turn it upside-down next to the fence and use it to clamber over to the other side, where I run down the path towards a paved road. In the distance I can hear the wail of a siren getting louder. It can't be for me though, surely – the police never arrive that fast. Do they? I pick up my pace while doing my best to look inconspicuous.

The only person I pass on my way to the station is a middle-aged woman walking a dachshund. She gives me a friendly greeting and her dog strains at the lead in its effort to come and sniff me, but I march on, neither acknowledging her nor breaking my stride. Despite trying to walk at a normal speed and avoid drawing attention to myself, I'm out of breath by the time I get to the platform. According to the display, the next train will be in five minutes, and I spend the time pacing restlessly back and forth, glancing constantly at the steps down to the platform. I know it's unlikely that the police would have launched a search this quickly, but even so, I'm relieved when the train pulls in and I can finally make my escape.

Once seated, I lean back against the headrest and close my eyes. The warmth of the carriage makes me drowsy. Only now as the tension eases and I start to relax do I realise how much this whole business has taken out of me. It's not every day you break into somebody's house, for goodness' sake. I'm about to drift off when I suddenly remember Alexander's note and am instantly awake. Where did I put the damn thing? It eventually turns up in my trouser pocket and I carefully smooth out the folds.

Once again, my eyes are drawn to the letters he ringed in the middle of the page: 'DNA'. This time, I also try to decipher what Alexander scribbled down alongside each of the arrows pointing away from the circle. 'Rain' I just about make out, and then 'evidence washed away', but no more than that. The rest of it doesn't amount to much without the relevant background knowledge, or else consists of abbreviations and acronyms I don't understand. I spend a while pondering what the letters 'IMTK?' might mean, which Alexander has underlined twice, but can't come up with anything that makes sense. Frustrated, I stuff the sheet back in my pocket, but my brain won't stop whirring.

Toni suddenly springs to mind. If I go about it the right way, maybe I can find out from her if David was in Berlin in the summer of 2003. The idea goes round and round in my head. I try to remember the last message she sent. Did she mention the name of the hospital she was staying in? Yes, she did – and also that she'd be there for a week. I sit bolt upright in my seat. There is a chance, of course, that she's already party to everything and won't want to talk to me. Even so, it's a risk I need to take.

The train stops in Schöneberg and I get out and ask for directions to the hospital. Drizzle sets in as I make my way over. The automatic glass doors glide open as I approach the entrance and I run my hands through my wet hair, hoping I don't look too conspicuous.

As soon as I enter the lobby, the standard hospital odour of pungent disinfectant wafts into my nostrils. I straighten up and head over to reception. The middle-aged woman behind the counter has obviously been to the tanning salon and her red-dyed pageboy bob glows pink under the fluorescent lighting.

'How can I help you?' She looks me up and down from behind her fashionably oversized spectacles without breaking her professional smile. Only the merest twitch in the corner of her mouth tells me that she doesn't rate my appearance too highly. Nonetheless, I force myself to meet her gaze. *Don't let her put you off.*

'A friend of mine is on the maternity ward here. I'd like to visit her, but can't remember what room she's in.' I give an apologetic shrug.

'Name?' Her voice sounds almost artificially generated. No modulation whatsoever.

I give her the information she needs and she turns back to her computer. Sharp, manicured fingernails clatter over the keyboard.

'Ah yes, there she is,' she says, and reaches for the phone. 'I'll let her know you're coming. What's your name?'

The urge to turn and run is powerful; it costs me the most enormous effort to remain standing calmly at the counter.

'Michaela Berger,' I reply, noting the obvious tremor in my voice.

'There's a Michaela Berger here to see you, Ms Wilhelmsen,' the receptionist warbles into the phone. She shoots me a suspicious sidelong glance while waiting for Toni's reply.

Every muscle in my body goes rigid and a pulse throbs away in my temples. I hardly dare to even breathe.

'I certainly will, Ms Wilhelmsen.' The receptionist hangs up.

Despite my jangling nerves, I put on a nonchalant air and even manage to flash the woman something resembling a smile.

'We're outside of visiting hours right now,' she informs me with a stern look, 'but your friend would like to see you nonetheless.'

'Oh, that's wonderful. Thank you so much,' I reply, feigning delight. 'Is she' – I hesitate briefly – 'alone? Or is her husband with her?'

'I'm afraid I don't have that information,' she replies, blinking primly.

Then she leans over the counter, granting me a close-up of her wrinkled cleavage, and points down the corridor to my left. 'Head through that door there, then follow the corridor and turn left at the end. Room forty-one.'

'Thanks,' I reply, before ambling along at a deliberately relaxed pace towards the entrance to the ward. It feels like the hardest thing I've ever done in my life. My hands are bunched into tense fists at my sides, my fingers so cramped I can hardly stretch them out. The glass door opens with a quiet swish when I hit the button and then slides shut behind me.

I know I can leave the ward through this door any time I like, but suddenly I feel trapped. I'm standing in a narrow corridor with apricot-coloured walls. It feels as though it goes on for ever. The pastel colours are probably designed to be soothing, broken only by the bright red fire extinguisher on the opposite wall. The floor is lined with pale linoleum that feels soft and slightly springy underfoot – like walking on cotton wool. Outside one of the rooms, I see an IV stand with a bag of transparent fluid dangling from it. It's uncomfortably warm in here and the scent of talcum powder hangs in the air. I have sickening flashbacks to my own stay in hospital fifteen years ago.

Back then, I suffered serious internal injuries in the accident and broke my pelvis in two places, leaving me bedbound for weeks. I had to do everything in bed – even wash myself and go to the toilet – while lying down or at best sitting up. If I'd had a private room, I probably wouldn't have found it so humiliating because, after all, nurses deal with that sort of thing every day. But the looks I got from my fellow patients – pitying or disgusted – were like torture. I never want to feel that helpless and vulnerable again. I'd rather die.

The urge to flee is so intense I actually turn round and start heading back towards the exit. A doctor in a white coat with a stethoscope around his neck approaches down the corridor and hurries past with a quick glance in my direction and a muttered greeting. I stop and watch him disappear around the corner, his coat billowing out behind him. If I leave now, I'll waste what will probably be my one and only chance to find out if David was in Berlin in the summer of 2003. Despite the anxious fluttering in my stomach, I force myself to get a grip. I can't keep running away when things get tough. And at last I find it: room forty-one.

21

I put my ear to the white-painted door and listen.

Silence.

What will you do if David's here? Run away?

I take a deep breath and knock.

'Come in,' a muffled voice answers.

Was that Toni? I can't be sure. My pulse quickens with anxiety. I push down the handle, open the door a crack and peer into the room. A strange odour drifts my way – sour somehow. It's not unpleasant exactly, but I've never come across anything like it before. Is this how newborn babies smell?

Toni is sitting by the window, wrapped in a pink terrycloth bathrobe. Her arms are cradling a white bundle of fabric framing a tiny rosy-cheeked face, his eyes closed. She looks worn out, but her eyes are glowing like she's the happiest person in the world.

'Come in!' she cries.

I do as she says and gently close the door behind me. She clearly has no idea of what's been going on or she'd never have greeted me so warmly.

'Hi, Toni,' I whisper.

'No need to whisper,' she says with a loud and hearty laugh. 'This little bundle of joy has just had his dinner and is sound asleep. He won't be waking up any time soon.'

'How lovely,' I say, unable to think of anything better. I'm painfully aware of how dreadful I look, but Toni seems too wrapped up in the baby to even notice.

'I'm so glad you came to see me. Isn't he gorgeous?'

'Yes, absolutely gorgeous,' I murmur, though privately I think the baby looks more like a monkey.

'The problem is I don't always have enough milk for him,' Toni patters on. 'The midwife says it'll sort itself out in time, but I'm a little worried about it myself.'

'That's understandable,' I reply. I suddenly feel completely out of place here.

How am I supposed to steer the conversation towards David? I can hardly ask her out of the blue, 'Hey, Toni, was your husband in Berlin in July 2003?'

'I happened to be in the neighbourhood and wanted to drop in and say hello,' I tell her. 'I can't stay long, I'm afraid.'

'That's a shame,' says Toni. 'David hasn't shown up today so far,' she adds somewhat curtly, 'and he's not even answering his phone. I expect he was out celebrating with his mates until all hours. He was absolutely over the moon – nearly bursting with pride,' she giggles. 'As if he made this little fellow happen all by himself!'

'I'm sure he'll turn up soon enough,' I mutter, guts churning.

'Could you do me a favour?' Toni lifts herself awkwardly from her chair.

Hesitantly I answer, 'Yeah, of course.'

'Can you hold him for a few minutes?' She lifts the baby bundle towards me. 'I want to take a quick shower before David gets here.'

'Oh, erm . . . sure,' I say, feeling like I've been ambushed. Timidly, I take the baby from her. She shows me how to support his little head and then hurries into the adjoining bathroom.

'I won't be long,' she promises, and closes the door behind her.

I stare down uneasily at the little pink face with his translucent eyelids and wrinkled forehead. The baby's hands are balled into tiny fists. He murmurs quietly in his sleep, bubbles of saliva forming between his lips. The idea comes out of nowhere, and then the plan takes shape in a matter of seconds.

I spring into action, as if I'm watching someone else. Carefully I tuck the warm bundle into the blue Moses basket next to the bed and then spread the blanket over the baby's tiny body. On the back of the catering menu lying on the table, I write:

*I'LL BRING YOUR BABY BACK IF DAVID MAKES
A FULL CONFESSION.*

There's the sound of running water in the bathroom. I pick up the basket and exit the room, closing the door softly behind me.

Luckily there's no one around on my way back to reception. Even the chair behind the counter is empty, so I make it out of the building unimpeded. As I hurry through the small park in front of the hospital, I notice a man walking towards me, head lowered, hands shoved in the pockets of his coat, with a large dressing on one cheek. David! A hot stab of alarm runs through me. Turning on my heel, I march back towards the hospital, but just outside the entrance I swing left across the rain-soaked lawn, expecting any second to hear David bellow my name and sprint after me. I pick up my pace, praying that the baby doesn't choose this precise moment to wake up and start bawling, but everything runs smoothly. I reach the road through a side exit and jog over to the nearby taxi rank. Wrenching open the door of the first car in the queue, I place the Moses basket on the back seat, then hurry round to the other side and climb in, slinging my backpack on the seat beside me.

'Where to then, young lady?' The driver – a middle-aged Turkish man whose German bears almost no trace of an accent – turns around to look at me with a friendly smile on his wrinkled face.

Shit. Where do I go with the baby? Not my mother's place, that's for sure. Or mine.

'Just a second,' I say, as I fumble in my coat for the business card.

Irena Kollar, Person-Centred Psychotherapist and Hypnotherapist, it says. The address is close by. I say the name of the road to the taxi driver, who nods, starts the engine and pulls away. I look back through the rear windscreen. All clear. Just as I'm about to turn away though, I notice a man sprinting over the grass towards the pavement. David! He stops, looking frantically in all directions. I duck down a little in my seat.

'Someone back there is waving at you, I think,' says the taxi driver, craning his neck. 'Should I stop?'

'No, no,' I answer, a touch too quickly. 'Drive on, please.'

'As you wish,' he replies, and flicks his indicator to turn on to a side road.

I wait until we've rounded the corner before I sit up again. In the rear-view mirror, I see two dark eyes flash me a questioning look. 'Everything OK?' he asks.

'Yep, fine thanks,' I reply, though nothing could be further from the truth. I feel like I'm inching closer to the abyss.

22

The rest of the journey takes place in silence, aside from occasional gurgles from the Moses basket. I glance down at him and wonder what the hell I was thinking. Kidnapping a newborn from a hospital – I must be completely out of my mind. I should turn round right now and take him back. Except then they'll arrest me, and I might never be able to prove who really murdered Alexander. I feel like throwing my hands up in despair.

'Are you sure you're all right?' Once again, the taxi driver's eyes bore into mine in the rear-view mirror.

'Yeah,' I reassure him. 'Why do you ask?'

'You just groaned like you might be feeling sick?' His voice lifts on the last word so it sounds like a question. He's probably worried I'm going to throw up all over his upholstery.

'No, no, I'm fine,' I reassure him. 'I just have a headache. I'll take something for it soon.'

With a flash of unease, I remember that nursing mothers aren't supposed to take painkillers, but the driver seems happy with my reply and turns his attention back to the road. Not long after, the car turns on to a residential street and slows down.

'Here we are,' the driver announces. 'What number did you want?'

'You can drop me off here,' I reply. 'It's only a short walk up the road.'

I lift my backpack on to my lap, unzip it, and while I'm fumbling for some cash, my fingers brush against something cold and smooth. I peer inside and lift out my purse. Underneath is the gun. I stare at it, thunderstruck. How did that get there? In my mind's eye, I run through the events by the lake. I tucked the gun into the top of my backpack, but then David must have got hold of it without my noticing and used it to shoot Alexander – or so I'd assumed until now anyway.

The sound of the driver clearing his throat drags me out of my bewildered state. I whip out my remaining banknote and press it into the man's hand, murmuring, 'Keep the change.'

'Oh, thanks!' he replies happily, and I realise I've paid him way too much.

I toss the purse back in the bag and scramble out on to the pavement. The idea of taking to my heels and simply leaving the Moses basket in the car flickers into my mind. It'd be better for me, I tell myself as I shoulder my backpack, and it'd certainly be better for the kid, but the man has already hopped out of the car, opened the rear door, taken out the basket and pressed it into my hand.

I don't have much choice but to take it.

'What a cute little thing,' he says, 'and still so tiny! Is it a boy or a girl?'

'A boy,' I say, forcing a smile. 'Thank you.' Then I turn and walk briskly off up the road.

I can feel his eyes on me and it takes every last shred of willpower not to look back. I hardly dare to breathe until I hear the car start up and pull away.

How am I going to explain my sudden appearance at Ira's place? I rack my brains as her building looms up ahead. The baby's growing restless, making smacking noises with his lips. He's clearly getting hungry and it won't be long before he starts crying. I walk faster and reach the front door just as a woman is pushing it open. Trying to act natural, I slip through behind her and slowly follow her up the steps. Ira's nameplate is on a door on the first floor. It's so big, you can't miss it. *Irena Kollar, Person-Centred Psychotherapist and Hypnotherapist.* I wonder whether Ira had ulterior motives when she gave me her card. Maybe she could sense there was something wrong with me, what with her training in psychology. The woman ahead of me rings Ira's doorbell. She must be one of her patients. What should I do? Go up a floor and wait until she's done? Before I've had time to make up my mind, Ira opens up and spots me straightaway.

'Michaela!' she cries, her voice filled with pleasure and surprise. Her eyes wander from my face to the Moses basket in my hand.

'Go on in, Heike. You know the way,' she says, turning with a friendly smile to the young woman, who pauses to give me the once-over. Ira steps to one side and Heike disappears into her apartment.

'Hi,' I manage to say before bursting into tears.

'Come on in.' Ira reaches for my hand, pulls me inside and shuts the door. 'I need to see to my client, but we'll talk after that. Make yourself at home in the living room until then, OK?' She points to a door. 'If you're thirsty, you'll find stuff in the kitchen. Just help yourself.'

She glances down at the baby, who once again is fast asleep.

'Boy or girl?' says Ira, asking the usual question.

'Boy,' I reply, gazing anxiously down at the baby's peaceful features.

'He's adorable,' Ira says.

'Yes,' I whisper plaintively.

She smiles, no doubt in an effort to cheer me up. She probably thinks I've run away from an abusive partner. I decide to let her believe what she likes for now.

'Can I use your phone?' I ask.

'Of course,' she replies. 'It's in the living room on the sideboard. Call whoever you like.'

'Thank you. Erm . . .'

Ira instantly grasps why I'm hesitating, though for all the wrong reasons, I presume.

'Don't worry,' she adds. 'Caller ID is switched off.'

The living room is typical for a Berlin apartment: large, with wooden floorboards and a three-panel window in the left-hand corner. The centre of the space is dominated by a vibrant red sofa with black cushions, and the walls around it are decked with carefully arranged abstract paintings, also in tones of red and black. An old-fashioned chandelier hangs from the ceiling. It looks like she found it in some flea market, as it doesn't quite match the rest of the furniture.

I place the basket on the sofa, sit down beside it and gently stroke the baby's soft cheek. He opens his eyes, blinks sleepily and makes sounds a bit like the quiet croaking of a frog. I wonder if I ought to pick him up. Just then, he opens his little mouth and gives an almighty yawn. He really is adorable. A surge of tenderness for this tiny helpless creature rushes through me, but the unfamiliar stirring instantly throws me into confusion and I leap to my feet.

23

I have no idea if directory enquiries still exists, but it's worth a try. I dredge up the old phone number from the dusty corners of my mind, enter it, and to my surprise actually hear a dial tone. Moments later, a friendly female voice asks what she can do for me and I request the number of the maternity hospital. 'No, I don't want to be connected, thank you,' I add before hanging up. Then I dial the number she gave me and hold the handset to my ear.

'Schöneberg Maternity Hospital, how can I help you?' From the monotonous voice, I realise I'm speaking to the same receptionist I met earlier.

'Could you please put me through to Antonia Wilhelmsen's room?' I try to make my voice sound different in the hope that she won't recognise me, but from the pause at the other end of the line, I can instantly tell she knows it's me. There's a babble of excited voices in the background.

'Ms Wilhelmsen hasn't booked a phone line for her room,' comes the eventual reply.

'Then bring her down to reception. I'll call back in a few minutes.'

'Wait, please—' I hear her breathless reply as I hang up.

Then I pace up and down the room clutching the phone. I'm sweating and only now do I notice that I'm still wearing my thick outdoor coat. I've well and truly screwed myself by kidnapping the baby. It's becoming ever clearer that I'm not going to get away with this. But before I hand myself in to the police, I need David to confess what he and his friend did all those years ago. Otherwise all this will have been in vain and I will once again be written off as a delusional female who thinks that every softly spoken blond man she claps eyes on is a murderer.

I press the redial button and somebody picks up on the first ring.

'Michaela!' Toni's sobbing into the receiver. 'What have you done with my baby? Where's Leander? Is he OK?'

'Yes, he's fine,' I say, and then after a brief pause I add, 'For now.' I don't like saying it – I don't want to scare her unnecessarily – but I need my demand to carry some weight. David has already experienced for himself how serious I am and what I'm capable of. I can only hope that he'll put the well-being of his infant son over his own.

While Toni struggles to breathe, I quickly continue. 'David needs to make a full confession, and then you'll get your baby back.'

'Ms Berger, it's time you saw sense,' an unfamiliar male voice suddenly declares down the line. 'Bring the child back to the hospital or tell us where you are right now, and then we'll—'

'I'm not talking to the police,' I say, cutting him off.

'Listen—' he objects.

'No! Put Toni or David on, or I'll hang up.'

There's further discussion in the background, but I can't make out what they're saying. Then David comes on the line.

'Listen to me, please,' he says. 'You've got some story into your head. I don't have a clue what you want from me.'

'Spare me the lies. You can't fool me,' I reply coldly.

'My God, I'm not trying to fool you! Why would I do that?'

'Because you don't want to spend the rest of your life behind bars?'

'Please be rational for a moment. You're rushing headlong into disaster and you're dragging us down with you.' He's resorted to pleading now, but I'm not falling for that either. He really should know me better by now.

'I want you to make a full written confession with every last detail,' I tell him, and hang up.

My stomach is on fire with all the tension. I'm worried that David is never going to admit what he did. When push comes to shove, he always puts himself first. He doesn't even seem to care about the life of his own child, or he would surely have given in to my demands this time round, if not before.

As if he can sense my nerves, the baby suddenly starts to scream. I pick him up, cradling his soft little head in my hand like Toni showed me, and wander around the room rocking him gently back and forth. He seems to like that, because he calms down again after a while, giving just the odd little squeal every now and then. My heart melts.

'There's nothing to be scared of,' I whisper. 'I won't hurt you. That's a promise.'

'Why would you hurt your own child?'

I freeze and then inch round. Ira is standing in the doorway with a deep frown on her face.

'I . . . Er . . .'

'That isn't your baby, is it?'

I try to say something, but nothing comes out.

24

I lower the baby back into the Moses basket and carefully tuck him in with the blanket. He looks up at me with wide, round eyes and stretches his little hands towards me as if he wants me to pick him up again. With a lump in my throat, I turn to look at Ira.

'No,' I say. 'It isn't my baby.' I have no idea why I'm telling her the truth; maybe I've just had enough of all the lies.

She purses her lips and nods several times, as if she was expecting me to say that. 'I think you owe me an explanation.' All trace of warmth has vanished from her voice. Her arms folded on her chest, she leans against the door frame and stares at me. I can't read her expression.

'Yes,' I say, gazing shamefaced at the floor. *Where on earth do I begin?*

And then the words start to pour out, as if I've been waiting for an opportunity to unburden my soul to someone. Ira listens, her face blank. She doesn't try to interrupt.

'I know it was insane, but . . .' I shrug and look up at her, silently begging for her understanding. 'Somehow there came a point when there was just no going back anymore. It was like I was in a trance.' It doesn't sound very convincing even to my own ears.

Ira doesn't say a word. She uncrosses her arms and walks past me, her entire demeanour cold and dismissive. I want the floor to open up and swallow me. Ira sits down on the sofa and leans over the Moses basket. She strokes the baby's cheek and a small smile flits over her face.

That only makes me feel more nervous. I instantly regret opening up to her. What was I thinking? I hardly know the woman. Suddenly I find myself longing for my mum; wishing I could take refuge in her protective embrace and have her reassure me that everything will be OK.

'From the moment we met, I could tell you were carrying a burden,' says Ira after a brief silence. 'You remind me of my daughter.' She looks me in the face. 'You have the same lost air about you. She was a drug addict. I tried everything, but I couldn't save her.'

'You mean, she passed away?' I ask in shock.

'Yes. She was always looking for the next high, as she put it.' Ira laughs bitterly. 'And yet her death was so low and sordid.'

'I'm so sorry.'

'It was a long time ago,' Ira answers tersely.

'I should probably leave,' I say.

'You're staying right here. We're not done yet.' A note of command has crept into her voice. I open my mouth to protest, but she carries on speaking. 'What makes you so sure you're right this time? That David and Leander really are one and the same person?'

'I recognised him, clear as day,' I reply. 'Besides, he called his baby Leander. That says it all.'

'No, it doesn't prove a thing.'

'And David shot Alexander because he thought he was Erik,' I counter.

'So you assume, but you don't know that for certain either. He claims it was you who killed Alexander.'

'Why would I do that?'

'Because he got in your way.' Ira's tone is more challenging now, as if she's waiting to see what I'll come out with in response.

And just then, with absolute horror, I remember the gun in my backpack. I told Ira that David shot Alexander with my pistol – and yet that can't have been how it happened. I swallow. My throat goes dry.

'You don't believe me,' I say.

'It doesn't matter if I believe you, Michaela. It's the police who need to believe you.'

'So what should I do?' My voice sounds every bit as desperate as I feel right now.

'You need to hand yourself in and tell them your version of events. If David did shoot Alexander, they'll find gunshot residues on him.'

'Gunshot residues?'

'That's right. They can detect microscopic particles to determine whether or not someone has fired a gun. And if you're wondering how I know that, my ex was a policeman. He liked lecturing me about his work, as well as being handy with his fists.' She rolls her eyes.

'But they'll find residues on me too. I shot at David.' I register Ira's look of horror. 'Just to scare him! I deliberately didn't aim at him,' I quickly add.

Ira frowns. 'Where did you learn how to shoot in any case?'

'From Robert, my mum's partner. He gave me lessons. He hunts and he's a member of a rifle club,' I mumble.

'Be that as it may, your reckless actions have landed you in a very difficult situation.' Ira stands up with a quiet sigh. 'Look, I'll drive you back to the hospital. This baby urgently needs to get back to his mother. The police will be on the scene by now too, so you can talk to them when we get there.'

Every fibre of my being is suddenly on red alert. If I hand myself in now, it'll all be over. David is clever – he'll twist things so that I end up as the guilty party. He'll claim he tried to grab the gun off me when

I shot Alexander. That would explain any gunshot residues on his body. The police will take his word over mine. To them, I'll be no more than a woman with mental health problems who's finally lost her marbles once and for all. They'll try me for a murder I never committed and David will get off scot-free yet again. I can't let that happen.

Where's my backpack? My eyes scan the room and I spot it on the floor by the sideboard.

Ira picks up the Moses basket. 'Shall we?'

I nod, pretending to go along with her, then grab my backpack and follow her out into the hallway. She's already shrugged on her coat and is wrapping a scarf around her neck.

'I'm not coming with you,' I say.

'What else are you going to do?'

'I don't know exactly, but I'm not going to the police. Not yet.'

'Michaela,' she says, blocking my path, 'you've kidnapped two people already and you're suspected of murdering a third.'

'Let me go,' I say.

'No!'

'Please.'

'No.'

'Then you leave me no choice,' I say.

The confusion on Ira's face gives way to an expression of shock as she stares in disbelief at the gun in my hand.

'Let me go,' I demand once again.

I can see her mind spinning through her available options. I hope she makes the right choice. I don't want to hurt her.

'Leave the baby here at least,' she entreats me.

I bite my lip and think it over, keeping a close eye on Ira. I wouldn't put it past her to try to overpower me, in spite of the gun. No, I need to take the baby with me. He's the only leverage I have left.

'Is that the gun Alexander was shot with?' Ira suddenly asks.

'Yes,' I reply, without stopping to think.

25

'Didn't you just say David stole it from you and used it to kill Alexander?' Ira's voice barely quivers, but I can still detect an undertone of fear.

'Well, yes,' I reply, 'that's what I thought, but—'

'So why do you still have it?' she cuts in.

It's a valid question – one I've also been racking my brains trying to answer ever since I found the gun in my backpack. I haven't found the solution yet, but then again, I have only very confused memories of what went on by the lake. It all happened so fast. Maybe Alexander had his service weapon with him, and maybe David used that to shoot him? I just don't know.

The only thing I can say with absolute certainty is that I wasn't the one who killed Alexander.

'I honestly don't know,' I reply. 'I thought David used my gun.'

'Something about your story doesn't add up,' Ira says, pursing her lips.

'Out of my way!' I say.

I lean forwards and snatch the Moses basket from her.

Ira backs away until she reaches the front door. 'I'm not letting you leave with the baby. You'll have to shoot me first.'

She lifts her chin bravely and spreads her arms across the door.

'Over my dead body,' she adds, in a remarkably firm voice.

I swallow and take off the safety catch. Ira flinches, but doesn't budge.

'Please, Ira,' I say, making one last attempt to defuse the situation, 'let me go.'

She shakes her head.

'They're going to throw me in jail – I don't stand a chance. Surely you must understand that,' I beg her.

'I have great faith in our justice system,' she says.

She sounds like my mother. Defiance wells up in me, but just as I'm about to come up with a retort, she adds, 'You can go, but the baby stays here.'

My mind starts racing. Leander will get hungry and start crying soon, and I won't have any way of calming him down. I'll attract a lot of attention carrying around a screaming baby. And the risk of someone recognising me is pretty high by now anyway. These days, the police in Berlin don't just broadcast a suspect's details on TV and over the radio, they use social media too.

'Fine,' I say, and put the Moses basket on the floor at my feet. Bang on cue, the baby starts to scream. 'I'll leave him here but I'm going.'

'You're making a mistake,' says Ira.

'Maybe so,' I reply.

'I can try to help you remember—'

Before she can go on, I silence her with a sweep of my hand.

'I know precisely what happened,' I reply. 'I don't need a psychologist for that. Now get out of my way.'

She still doesn't move.

'Please, Ira. You promised you'd let me go if I left the baby here.'

Reluctantly she steps aside. 'This isn't the right choice,' she says, before adding quietly, 'You're making a huge mistake, Michaela. Please – stop and think it through.'

Biting my bottom lip to stop myself from bursting into tears, I shake my head. Then I leave Ira's apartment without looking at her. She doesn't try to stop me.

I shut the door behind me and walk down the stairs and out on to the street. Chances are that Ira is already on the phone to the police. Just then, a look of panic on the face of a passer-by reminds me that I'm still brandishing the gun. I quickly stuff it in my backpack, pull my hood over my head and walk on. I need to get out of here fast. The din of passing traffic engulfs me, until suddenly a police siren strikes up, drowning out everything else. My pulse quickens. I spot the blue sign of a U-Bahn station over the road and make a dash for it, not stopping to look left or right. Brakes squeal and someone bellows at me, but I pay no heed and rush on towards the station entrance. A gust of wind catches my hood and blows it back as I totter down the steps. I hear the rumble of a train coming into the station and pick up my pace. The lights over the doors change from green to red just as I make it on to the platform. Running as hard as I can, I dive into the nearest carriage and hear the beep as the doors slide shut behind me.

Breathing heavily, I collapse into an empty seat. I'm in such a state, my whole body is jangling with nerves. It takes quite a while until my head clears and I can see my next step.

There's only one person who knows the whole truth. I need to find him – even if every single part of me rebels at the thought.

26

By the time a tide of bodies washes me out of the station at Schlesisches Tor and on to the street, it's already dark. Coloured fairy lights blink and flash from the surrounding storefronts. A sticker of a chubby-faced Santa Claus grins at me from a nearby window in front of a sparkling display. That's right, it's nearly Christmas. I'd completely forgotten – though I don't think I've ever felt less Christmassy than I do right now. I thrust my hands into my coat pockets, scurry across the road and head down Skalitzer Strasse. Here too, lights in red, green, yellow and blue glitter and flash behind the windows of the apartment blocks lining the road.

For a moment, the urge to flee home to my apartment is so overwhelming that I'm tempted to give in to it. The only thing stopping me is the fear that the police might be ready and waiting to arrest me on the spot.

I'm utterly exhausted and longing for my bed. Right now, I would give an awful lot to be able to rewind the last few days and go back to my boring everyday life. I should have gone to the police with my suspicions. So what if they think I'm crazy? In hindsight, I can't even explain to myself any more what possessed me to kidnap David. It was pure insanity. What the hell was I thinking? No idea. Not that it matters. All that's left is the bitter understanding that I'm to blame for Alexander's death. Not directly, admittedly, but that doesn't make it any better. I can't let David get away with this. It's the least I owe to poor Alexander.

I'm so lost in thought, I almost walk past the building. The windows on the third floor are dark. David doesn't seem to be home. I hold back for a moment, but then pluck up my courage and start pushing doorbells at random.

'Yes?' a male voice barks into the intercom.

'Leaflets,' I reply, and the door buzzes open.

The building feels hostile. Cold, damp air wafts towards me from the interior. There's a sickly sweet odour reminiscent of rotten fruit. The 'OUT OF ORDER' sign is still taped to the lift door. It's like the building is doing its utmost to try to stop me from paying a call on David.

Slowly, step by step, I climb the stairs, my right hand gripping the smooth wooden banister. The closer I get to the third floor, the less sure I am of myself.

You can still turn round and leave.

And what then? Go into hiding? Leave Germany and flee to another country? Neither option strikes me as a good solution. On the third floor, I take a deep breath and ring the bell, but the door remains firmly shut. It seems like David really isn't home. He's probably still with Toni at the hospital. If I'm really unlucky, he'll spend the night there too. I ring the bell again. When no one comes on the third attempt, I decide to hunker down and await his return.

To retain the element of surprise, I take a seat on the stairs one floor up, with my backpack on the step beside me. The light in the stairwell goes out with a quiet click. I drag myself wearily to my feet, press the switch – which glows like a red eye in the darkness – and then shuffle back to where I was sitting.

A sudden whim prompts me to dig out the page from Alexander's notepad from my pocket. If only I knew what 'IMTK?' meant. I can't shake the feeling that this sequence of characters contains an important message – especially as it's the only thing on the page that Alexander underlined. But however much I puzzle over the conundrum, I can't make head nor tail of it.

The light goes out again. This time I don't bother to switch it on. I stuff the paper back into my pocket, prop my arms on my legs and close my eyes. The cryptic letters on Alexander's notepad drift through my mind before suddenly whirling together and arranging themselves in a different order – though not one that makes any sense, unfortunately. My eyelids grow heavy and keep drooping shut. I'm just on the point of nodding off when the stairwell is suddenly flooded with light.

I'm instantly wide awake. The sound of heavy footsteps echoes through the silence. Is it David? My heart starts beating faster. I stand up, grab my backpack and lean over the banister to peer downstairs.

The steps draw closer. I can hardly bear the tension. Only when the person reaches the final flight of steps leading up to the third floor do I finally catch a glimpse of him. It's David alright. He looks totally shattered; he's dragging his feet. The last few days have obviously taken their toll.

My hand trembles as I fish the gun out of my backpack, but I force myself to stay calm. I can't let him see me too early.

27

I wait for David to push his key into the lock of his front door, then dash down the steps. Before he has a chance to grasp what's happening, I jam my gun into his back.

'Make a noise and you're dead,' I hiss. I feel like a character from some schlocky thriller, but it works.

A jolt passes through his body. He hesitates briefly, then steps into his apartment without saying a word. I follow close behind, shoving the door shut with my foot once I'm through. It falls into the latch with a clunk. Waving the gun, I gesture for David to take a seat on the living room sofa and then park myself down opposite. He stares at me with bloodshot eyes. There's something in his expression I can't quite place. If I didn't know better, I'd say it was pity. He looks like he's aged by several years. We stare at each other for a while. Eventually he breaks the silence.

'What do you want from me?' His voice is hoarse.

'That really should be obvious to you by now,' I reply. 'I've said it often enough.'

'Toni told me what happened all those years ago.' His eyes wander back to the gun in my hand. 'Can't you put that thing away? You're making me nervous, quite honestly.'

'What did she tell you exactly?' I ignore his request and keep the gun trained on his chest.

'How your friends were murdered by that lake.' He rubs his nose with the back of his hand and then looks at the floor, as if he's suddenly embarrassed to meet my gaze. 'You were the only one who managed to get away.'

'And nobody knows that better than you,' I reply. It costs me some effort to keep my voice level. His brazenness is astonishing.

'Michaela . . .' It's the first time he's ever said my name. He looks me straight in the eye. 'The detective at the hospital told me this isn't the first time you've falsely accused someone. But it sounds like you've never gone this far before with anyone else. You're not well, Michaela. You need help.'

Who does he think he is exactly? Leander, of all people, trying to tell me *I'm* not well. I'm so angry I could scream in his face, but it's like I'm paralysed.

'You're wrong this time too, believe me. I had nothing to do with that awful crime.'

Fortunately I soon recover myself. 'You might fool Toni. She loves you and doesn't have much choice but to believe you, or else her perfect little world would fall apart. But you can't pull the wool over my eyes. I know you murdered my friends. You and your chum Felix.'

'I've never had a friend called Felix,' David insists, wringing his hands as he speaks. 'All I can tell you yet again is that you've got the wrong idea.'

'Well, that's not his real name, of course,' I retort. 'Just like yours isn't Leander.' I take off the safety catch and aim the gun at David's face.

David shrinks back and holds up his hands. 'I can prove I wasn't in Berlin in summer 2003,' he says quickly.

I pause. This is a trap. He's planning something. All my senses go on high alert.

'I'd like to see you try,' I reply with studied indifference, but an uneasy feeling settles in my belly. He seems so certain he's got the edge over me.

'The proof is in the sideboard over there.' He turns his head and points over to his right.

I follow his gaze to a large white metal cabinet, which takes up half the wall. On it stands a slim vase made of clouded glass with a single red rose in it. Probably artificial, though it looks incredibly realistic.

'Go on,' I say. My curiosity gets the better of my fear.

David gets up from the sofa and I do the same, keeping a close eye on him. There might be a gun hidden in the sideboard. He opens one of the doors and takes out a large book. On second glance, I realise it's a photo album.

'These are the pictures from every holiday I took with my parents. They put this album in one of my removal boxes when I moved up here.' He puts it down on the table and starts leafing through.

The whisper of the parchment paper jangles on my nerves. My mouth is so dry, I can barely swallow.

'Here it is.' He taps his finger on the open page.

'Give it here,' I bark at him.

He removes the photo from beneath the plastic sheet and hands it to me.

'Sit back down,' I tell him. He does what I say without protest.

The photo shows a mutinous-looking teenager flanked by two adults who are grinning broadly for the camera. All three figures are wearing outdoor clothes and standing in front of a wooden cross marking the summit of a mountain. In the background, an Alpine landscape spreads out beneath a brilliant azure sky. The boy bears an uncanny resemblance to Leander – tall, skinny and blond, with acne scarring his cheeks and forehead – but it's unmistakably David. It feels as though a veil is being lifted from my eyes.

'My parents were into hiking,' he says flatly. 'Unlike me.'

Without taking my eyes off David, I pull the album towards me. On the page he took the photo from, someone has written in crisp, neat handwriting:

July 2003 – Holiday in Kleinwalsertal, Austria, with Simone and David.

'My father was a teacher,' says David. 'We spent the whole of July there, as well as the first week of August. My mother's still alive; she can confirm it. I can call her right now if you like.'

28

David reaches into his pocket and pulls out his phone.

'Leave it,' I hiss.

'As you wish.' He tucks it away again.

This can't be possible. I feel sick. The photo slips through my fingers and sails to the floor. The world suddenly turns grey before my eyes and I cling to the sideboard for support. David could easily overpower me right now, but he doesn't move from where he's sitting.

'So why did you shoot Alexander?' My voice sounds uncertain.

'That wasn't me,' he replies.

'You're lying.'

'No,' he insists. 'All of a sudden there was a bang and Alexander dropped to the ground. You must have shot him. There was no one else around.'

'No!' I gasp. 'Why would I have shot him?'

'Maybe' – a sly expression creeps over David's face – 'because he wanted to reopen the case? Isn't that what he said? Maybe you're the one with something to hide.'

'You shut your mouth!' I yell at him.

'Why don't you turn yourself in at last? The police know your name and they're looking for you everywhere. You don't stand a chance. If you give yourself up, it'll count in your favour. Be reasonable. Come on, give me the gun.' David leans forwards and holds out his hand. 'Pretty please?' His eyes flash with a treacherous gleam. I still don't trust him an inch.

'No way!' I shake my head furiously. Pointing my revolver at him again, I start to retreat towards the door.

'Don't make things any worse than they already are,' he says pleadingly. 'There's no way out for you now.'

I glance over my shoulder to make sure I'm moving in the right direction.

'Put your phone on the floor and kick it towards me,' I instruct him.

He hesitates, then does as I say. The phone rattles over the floor-boards. I pick it up and keep heading for the door, then quickly snatch the key from the lock, slam the living room door behind me and lock it from the outside. It won't give me more than a brief head start, though I don't actually know what my next move should be. David's phone is password-protected and therefore unusable, so I turn the sound off and leave it on the shelf over the coat rack.

I'm nearly at the foot of the stairs when it hits me that I've left my backpack in David's apartment. Unfortunate, but there's not much I can do about it now. I tuck the gun in my pocket and totter down the three steps leading from the main entrance on to the street. The world starts spinning before my eyes; I feel like I'm going to pass out at any moment. I brace myself against a streetlight as a train rumbles past on the tracks overhead. Somewhere nearby, a driver leans on their car horn.

David didn't murder my friends. I've got the wrong man. Again. My cheeks burn with shame. What on earth have I done, in my frantic obsession with finding Leander? My surroundings blur as the tears well up. I wipe my eyes, then pull myself together when I notice passers-by giving me odd looks. I need to get out of here.

My gun disappears into a bin at the next pedestrian crossing. I don't want it any more. Snatches of broken thoughts whirl around my head as I hurry through the streets. I need to talk to someone before I lose my mind completely.

Something happened by the lake, just before Alexander was shot. The thought suddenly forms on the edge of my consciousness, but slips away again before I can properly focus on it.

All my energy is gone now; I have to virtually drag myself onwards. The air is ice-cold and burns the inside of my lungs. I can barely feel my fingers, and the last few yards to my mother's apartment block are pure torture. After what seem like long oceans of time, I come to a halt and cast my eyes over the front of the building. The windows on the second floor are blazing with light. She's at home, thank God. Hopefully Robert's not with her. He's the last person I want to see right now.

I ring the doorbell. Her voice emerges from the intercom so fast you'd be forgiven for thinking she'd been stationed by the front door all this time, listening out for me.

'Mum, it's me,' I whisper.

The door buzzes open before I'm even done speaking and I rush into the lobby before it slams shut behind me with a bang. My whole body's trembling from the cold as I haul myself up the stairs. Mum is standing in the doorway waiting for me, her face wet with tears. Wordlessly she pulls me into her flat and takes me into her arms. I rest my head on her shoulder and some of the strain I've been under starts to melt away. It'll all be OK, I think – though I know that's an illusion. Nothing will ever be the same again. I can't face that possibility right now, however; I'd sooner ignore any negative thoughts and feelings. For a while, we simply stand there and hold each other, until in the end Mum lets me go. She wipes her cheeks with both hands and fixes me with a smile, though it looks strained and desperate.

'You're hurt,' she says, stroking my cheek gently.

'It's not so bad,' I reply, feeling like a helpless child. 'I'd almost forgotten about it.'

'I'm going to run you a bath before we even start to think of anything else,' she says. 'You look frozen to the bone.'

'But shouldn't we talk about—?'

'Later,' she says, cutting me off. 'We have all the time in the world.'

Her words take me by surprise, but I don't try to argue. I simply don't have the energy. I hang my coat on the rack and follow her into the bathroom. She turns on the taps and sprinkles bath salts into the tub while I start to peel off my clothes. The room fills with steam and the soothing scent of lavender. I climb into the bath, slip gently into the warm water and close my eyes with a sigh of relief. Mum shuts the door softly behind her.

The warmth makes me sleepy and my eyelids start to flutter, then droop.

A silhouette suddenly emerges from the clouds of steam in the air. To my horror, I realise it's Alexander – his face one huge crater filled with blood and gore.

Just a dream, it's just a dream, my rational mind tells me, but the feeling of dread refuses to leave me.

Alexander raises his hand and points at me. A chill, hollow voice echoes through the bathroom, bringing me out in goosebumps and burrowing deep into my brain.

IMTK, it whispers. *IMTK.*

29

I sit up with a jolt. The bathwater has cooled by several degrees and my whole body is covered in goosebumps. There's a knock at the door, and for one fearful moment I worry that my mum might have taken the opportunity to call the police.

'These will probably be a bit big for you, but at least they're clean and dry.' She places a stack of neatly folded clothes on the stool next to the bath.

'Oh, thank you,' I reply, lifting myself out of the tub.

'I'll be in the living room,' she says, and then as she heads back out, 'Robert just got here, by the way.'

Before I have a chance to remonstrate, she closes the door behind her.

Why didn't she tell him to leave? She knows perfectly well that I don't like him much. The very idea of seeing him now makes me uncomfortable. He'll doubtless bombard me with questions and then tell me that my crackpot scheme was the most idiotic thing I could ever have done. And he'll be right unfortunately. I dry myself thoroughly to put off the unwanted encounter for as long as possible.

Wiping the condensation from the mirror with my hand, I note that the scratch on my cheek has finally scabbed over. My eyes are bloodshot, my face is alarmingly pale – almost grey in hue – and my wet hair clings to my neck like a tangle of snakes. I'm not exactly a beauty at the best of times, but I've never looked quite this bad before. In any case, my appearance is a pretty close approximation of how I feel. Taking a deep breath, I open the bathroom door.

There's someone coughing in the living room. It sounds like an elderly dog barking. Robert has asthma; it gets especially bad when he's stressed or excited.

He and my mother are whispering to each other as I enter the room, but stop when they see me. They look up at me sombrely, two little faces side by side on the couch.

'Hello, Michaela,' says Robert. I can see at a glance that he's up to speed with everything.

'Hello, Robert.' I remain standing in the middle of the room. There's an atmosphere here, but I can't quite put my finger on it. I'm getting more nervous by the moment.

'Why don't you sit down?'

'I'd rather not,' I reply.

The two of them exchange a glance and my mother clears her throat.

'I don't know where to start,' she says, wringing her hands.

'Are the police on their way?' I ask. 'Is that what you're trying to tell me?'

'Oh no, sweetheart,' Mum reassures me, then pauses again awkwardly. 'It's about Alexander. . .'

'Alexander?' I repeat dully, and decide to sit down after all. I don't need to be psychic to know this won't be good news.

'How should I tell her?' She looks helplessly at Robert. He reaches for her hand and she gives him a weak smile.

'Alexander turned up in the shop the day before yesterday,' she says.

I gnaw my bottom lip, feeling awkward. 'I lied to you, Mum. I'm sorry.'

She doesn't acknowledge my apology, but carries on talking, her eyes fixed on her hands as they fiddle with the hem of her blouse. 'I knew even before he came that you'd lied to me and that you were up to some ridiculous scheme or other. I'd just found what you'd ordered online. I was about to tell Robert when the door of the shop opened and there was Alexander.' She clears her throat and tucks a strand of hair behind her ear.

'I didn't know he was a policeman. He only told me later. Otherwise I'd obviously have kept my hunch to myself that you might have taken Toni's husband to the lake.'

She looks me in the eye and her expression of despair shocks me to the core.

'That was when he told me there were new leads in the case and he wanted to reopen it. Though he didn't tell me exactly what that meant.'

'But it's good they want to look into everything again,' I say. 'Maybe the truth will finally come out.'

Once again, my mum fixes me with that strange, sad look. Her eyes fill with tears. She swallows, clearly finding it hard to go on. 'Alexander said he knew where the lake was and that he'd go straight there to save you from your own stupidity.'

Every word that comes out of her mouth makes me feel worse. I'm ashamed at myself for causing her so much heartache.

'As soon as he left the shop, I called Robert and told him everything.'

'You looked up the location of the lake online, remember? Your mother gave me the directions and I headed straight there,' says Robert.

'But why? Alexander was already on his way.'

'Well, I—' A coughing fit prevents him from saying any more.

Mum springs to her feet and fetches his asthma inhaler from the drawer. Robert takes a puff and then continues hoarsely with his account.

'I had a bad feeling. I just wanted to . . .' He trails off, as if unsure of what to say.

'It was my fault,' says Mum. 'I was sure Alexander knew more than he was letting on. You could tell just by looking at him. I was absolutely beside myself – I feared the worst. Robert drove to the lake because I asked him to.'

'What do you mean? What were you afraid of?' I ask. Feeling deeply uneasy by now, I look first at her, then at Robert. 'Why are you speaking in riddles?'

30

The two of them avoid my eye, remaining studiously silent. Eventually Robert opens his mouth.

'It wasn't hard to see which path you took from the car park. You left clear enough tracks.'

That bark I heard in the woods – it was Robert coughing, I realise with a jolt.

'I took my rifle with me, just in case.'

'In case of what?'

'I didn't know what was happening between you. Whether you might need help.'

Mum pulls out a handkerchief and noisily blows her nose. She can't seem to stop crying. Robert gives her a gentle pat on the arm before going on.

'I listened to the three of you for a while. When that policeman told you he'd come across some inconsistencies in the original murder investigation, I thought, *Oh, it's bound to come out now. We'll all end up behind bars.* The very idea made me cough. Only briefly, but it was enough. He saw me. And then . . . I somehow couldn't help it. I pulled the trigger.'

'You mean, *you* killed Alexander?'

Robert can't look me in the eye.

'Mum,' I say, staring at her helplessly, 'please tell me it's not true!'

She breaks out in sobs, pressing the crumpled handkerchief to her mouth.

'But why? I . . . I don't understand any of this.'

'All those years ago, I was the one who cleaned out your mother's car – the one you were driving when you had your accident – before it was scrapped.' Robert's voice sounds oddly tinny. 'I found a gun under the passenger seat and I put it in my pocket.'

'A gun? Under the passenger seat?' I stare at him in disbelief.

Mum clears her throat and wipes the tears from her cheeks. 'Straightaway we realised what had really happened by the lake.' She looks at me now, as if begging for forgiveness. 'We had to protect you. You're my baby, aren't you? I couldn't just let them—'

At long last, I manage to collect myself and cut her off. 'You mean, you've spent all these years believing it was me who killed Paul and the others?'

'All the evidence seemed to point that way,' says Robert gravely.

'I have no idea how that gun got into the car,' I say, 'but there's one thing I'm certain of: I didn't kill anyone.' I bite my lip to stop myself from bursting into tears. 'How could you even think I'd do such a thing?'

'You were completely beside yourself, my love. I barely recognised you. You were so torn up with the pain of Paul leaving you and your jealousy towards Maike.'

'I loved Paul – I would never have done anything to hurt him.'

My mother reaches across the table to take my hand, but I instinctively pull it back and shove it under my thigh.

'It pains me to say it, but you seemed almost out of your mind back then. Robert and I even wondered if we ought to have you temporarily admitted to a psychiatric clinic.'

'My God, I was eighteen!' I say, shaking my head in bewilderment. 'I was truly in love for the first time in my life. Of course I was suffering – of course I thought it was the end of the world. I'll admit I even thought about killing myself at times. That's how teenagers react. It's a hormonal thing; everyone knows that.' By now I've worked myself up into a rage. I dart furious looks at Robert and my mother.

'You couldn't remember any details to begin with after the accident,' she goes on.

'And? What's that supposed to mean?' I sound more petulant than I mean to, but I can't get round how deeply hurt I am that my own mother thinks I'm capable of murdering my friends in cold blood.

'The doctor blamed the gaps in your memory on amnesia as a result of the concussion you suffered in the accident. He said it'd wear off soon enough.'

'But after I found the gun in your car,' Robert says, picking up the story, 'your mother and I realised that your subconscious mind was doing its best to hide the fact that you yourself had murdered Paul and his friends.'

I can hardly bear the pitying looks on their faces. I'm on the verge of screaming. They're making me feel guilty for a crime there's no way I could have committed.

'You had terrible nightmares after the accident,' my mother continues. 'You'd cry out in your sleep and kept talking about a gun.'

'But why? I don't understand,' I murmur.

'Once, you sat bolt upright in bed, stared at me with your eyes wide open and whispered, "I'm innocent. It was Leander and Felix. They did it." I lost count of the number of times you repeated those words in your sleep over the following nights.'

'But it's true.' I can hardly get the words out.

'My love, those two boys only exist in your imagination.'

I shake my head. 'No, you're wrong. Why would I have invented them?' I ask desperately, though the answer is obvious.

'We spent a long time trying to work out what might have driven you to commit such a dreadful crime, but' – Robert shrugs – 'we could only guess at your true motives. All the same, we agreed that you needed to repress the memory of what you'd done in order to go on living.'

'The police never found Leander and Felix of course, because they simply don't exist,' my mother adds, somewhat unnecessarily.

Can the two of them really be talking about me? It suddenly seems as though nothing they're saying is getting through. I sit there, watching their lips move, form words and sentences, and feel like I'm in a silent movie to which someone has forgotten to add the subtitles.

Only when I hear someone saying my name loudly do I come back to myself. 'Huh? Sorry?'

'We need to figure out what to do next,' says Robert. 'You'll need to turn yourself in. They'll charge you with the kidnapping, if nothing else.'

It's absurd, I know, but I have to press my lips together to stop myself from laughing. If only he knew that I'd kidnapped Toni's baby too. Oh God, I really am losing my mind here. *Pull yourself together.*

'At least they can't pin Alexander's murder on you because he wasn't killed with your gun,' Robert says reassuringly.

'You sound like you couldn't care less that a man is dead – or that you were the one who killed him. What were you thinking? Did you picture yourself aiming at some stag on one of your hunting trips or something? This beggars belief!' The words come pouring out as if it's not me speaking, but someone else.

'He did it for you,' my mother says in a choked voice. Robert looks at the floor.

'For me?' I reply scornfully.

'Yes, for you,' she sobs.

'And you really believe that? I think he did it for himself, because he was worried the police might get wind of the fact that he hid an apparent murder weapon all those years ago.'

'Michaela, please,' she pleads, but I can't stop.

'I saw you, by the way,' I say accusingly, turning on Robert. 'At Alexander's house. What were you doing there?'

Judging by the surprise on my mother's face, this is news to her.

Robert's face turns red. 'I took the case file from the house and destroyed it,' he admits slowly.

'And what if there are copies? What will you do then?' I stand up abruptly. I need to get out of here – I can't take another second in their toxic company.

'Where are you going?' my mother asks in alarm.

'Away,' I reply, before storming out of the room.

At the last second, I remember to grab my coat from its hook. On an impulse, I also decide to pocket the spare keys to my apartment, which I find hanging on the rack.

Mum has followed me into the hall. 'Please, Michaela, don't run off. Let's talk rationally about this.'

I stop on the threshold and slowly turn round. She looks so desperate and unhappy that I'd like nothing more than to take her into my arms. But then Robert appears and my insides turn to stone.

'Talk about what? You're obviously both convinced I'm a murderer.'

Robert stands beside my mother and puts his arm around her. 'Where will you go?'

The fear that I might run straight to the police with his confession is written all over his face. Wordlessly I turn and leave the apartment.

No one tries to stop me.

31

The icy wind hits my blazing cheeks like a slap. I pace the streets without really taking in my surroundings. Eventually I find myself back at the bin where I disposed of my gun earlier and fish about under the lid. Gingerly I pull the pistol out and tuck it into the roomy inside pocket of my coat. It feels heavy somehow, as if it's put on weight over the last few hours. The only gun I've ever had in my possession is this one. My father's old revolver. This pistol is proof that I'm not a murderer. But what am I supposed to do with that knowledge? I can't go reporting my own mother and her partner to the police – everything they did was for my sake, after all, even though it was wrong.

I trudge onwards, increasingly overcome by despair. I want to go home. My hand closes over the keys in my coat pocket. It's worth a try. The police will have already searched my apartment and moved on.

But what if they're watching the building?

There's only one way to find out. I quicken my pace.

My mother's accusation is still reverberating through my brain. I didn't just imagine Felix and Leander. That's impossible. I can call Leander to my mind's eye in a snap, so vividly do I remember what he looks like. What about Felix though? I've only ever really had the vaguest impression of him, which somehow never coalesced into a complete picture. But that doesn't mean a thing. Leander is imprinted on my memory because I was so terrified of him and his soft voice, which contrasted so violently with his brutal actions. Yet that explanation suddenly rings hollow.

Robert's voice whispers in my ear: *You needed to repress the memory of what you'd done in order to go on living.*

That's just not true. It's not how it happened at all. I'm no murderer. I flinch – did I just say that out loud? I glance surreptitiously at the people around me, but no one pays me the slightest bit of attention. Soon afterwards, I turn on to the street where I live. The water sloshes gently against the walls of the Landwehr Canal. Light shines from some of the windows on the surrounding buildings, and the narrow road lies deserted under the dull glow of the streetlights. Nothing out of the ordinary.

I walk past my building, peering into each one of the parked cars. When I reach the end of the street, I cross and walk back down the other side. A light flickers behind a windscreen. Was that a match being lit? I look more closely and see the outlines of two people, along with the glowing tip of a cigarette. So they are keeping an eye on the place after all. My heart starts pounding as if it's about to explode. I lower my head and walk on. My pulse only settles once I've turned back on to the busier main road, where I feel sure the two police officers can't see me.

So what now? There's no way I'm going back to my mother's. A café maybe? I don't have any cash left though.

As if that weren't enough, it starts to snow. Shivering, I hunch my shoulders and shove my cold hands into my coat pockets. Wait – what's that? Next to the spare keys to my flat, I find a car key. I must have grabbed both of them in my rush to leave earlier. A flurry of snow blows into my face. The weather's getting worse. It doesn't take long to reach a decision and I turn and walk briskly back to my mother's apartment.

Her car is easy enough to find, fortunately – it's bright red and stands out like a beacon among all the dark and silver cars parked on the road. I unlock it and get in. The windows are steamed up and it's just as chilly inside as out on the street. With fingers stiff from the cold, I put the key in the ignition, start the engine and drive off. After a while, I realise I'm in Ira's neighbourhood; my subconscious mind has clearly led me back here, though I doubt her offer to help me still stands. After all, I threatened her with a gun and she knows I'm wanted by the police. Even so, she's the only person I have left to turn to.

A car pulls away as I reach Ira's building – a good omen. All the same, I remain sitting indecisively at the wheel, watching snowflakes coat the windscreen in a layer of white and gradually block my view of the outside world. For a moment, cocooned from my surroundings like this, I feel safe and protected, but after a few minutes the cold creeps in and I start to shiver.

I get out, stretch my stiff limbs and then climb the steps up to the entrance of the building. It's several minutes before Ira's voice emerges from the intercom.

'It's me – Michaela,' I mumble, feeling so self-conscious I can barely open my mouth.

'Sorry, who did you say?' asks Ira. She sounds confused.

'It's Michaela,' I say again, a little louder this time.

Silence from the other end of the line. Did she just hang up without saying a word?

Well, what were you expecting? That she'd welcome you with open arms? A dead weight of disappointment settles on my chest.

I turn to leave and am nearly at the foot of the steps when the buzzer sounds to let me in. On reaching the first floor, I find

Ira waiting for me in the entrance to her apartment, arms folded, her eyes watchful and face impassive.

'What do you want?' she asks coldly.

'I don't have anywhere else to go,' I reply. It sounds more pathetic than I'd like, but it clearly has an impact. Ira's grim expression softens slightly.

'OK,' she says hesitantly, 'come in.'

'Thank you,' I reply and step into the hallway, where I wait expectantly as Ira closes the door behind me.

'I was hoping you'd turn yourself in,' she says.

'I . . . It's just . . .' I mumble, unsure of how or where to start.

'Take your coat off first,' she says, 'then we'll sit down and talk about it, OK?'

I peel my coat off, but as I do so, the pistol falls out of the inside pocket and clatters to the floor.

Ira shrinks back, her eyes wide.

'Don't worry,' I say quickly, 'you can have it. I only need it to prove that it wasn't me who shot Alexander.'

Ira takes me at my word. She picks the gun up by her fingertips, places it in a drawer under the coat rack and shuts it firmly. Then she beckons me to follow her. The TV's on in the living room. A newsreader is gazing into camera with a grave expression. His lips are moving, but the sound is muted.

'Take a seat,' Ira says. She picks up the remote control and turns off the TV, then sits down opposite and fixes me with a questioning look. I swallow. Where on earth do I start?

'You mentioned that you might be able to help me shed light on the dark corners of my memory,' I say in the end.

'What's happened?'

'I've made a mistake.' I lace my fingers together for comfort. It's so hard to admit this, I can barely even get the words out. 'It turns out that . . . David – my friend's husband,' I add, by way of explanation, 'is not Leander after all.'

'I suspected as much,' Ira replies, a note of compassion in her voice.

I chew my bottom lip, gather all my courage and ask weakly, 'Do you think it's possible that Leander and his friend Felix only exist in my imagination?'

32

Silence.

I manage to tear my eyes away from my hands in my lap and gaze directly into Ira's face. She gives me a long and thoughtful look.

'Yes,' she says slowly, 'it certainly is possible. What makes you think that might be the case?'

'It doesn't matter,' I reply.

'Michaela, if you don't trust me, I can't help you.'

'I can't tell you. My mother would . . .' I pause and shrug helplessly. 'Maybe it's better if I leave.' I start to get up.

'No, stay. Please.' Ira gets to her feet. 'You can sleep in the spare room. We'll talk it over in the morning.'

'Thank you,' I say with tears in my eyes.

'Now don't get me wrong,' she adds, 'this isn't a free pass. I still think you need to go to the police and take responsibility for what you've done.'

I nod and whisper, 'I just want to know what really happened by the lake all those years ago.'

'We can try to find out through hypnosis,' says Ira, 'but I can't promise it'll work first time. The truth might be buried so deep inside that we can't access it. And if we do . . .' She pauses. 'It's possible that you won't like what gets washed to the surface.'

'I'll take my chances,' I reply, though a shiver runs down my spine.

Ira shows me to her guest room – a narrow room with a single bed and a pine wardrobe. It's a little spartan, but at least it's somewhere I can feel safe for the night. She presses some bedding into my hand, shows me the bathroom and wishes me good night.

'Thank you, from the bottom of my heart,' I say, when she turns to leave the room.

'I'm probably making a big mistake.' She twists her mouth into a smile. 'Like I said, it's lucky for you that you remind me of my daughter.'

She closes the door behind her. Out of nowhere, I find myself wishing she would stay with me until I fall asleep, and I'm briefly tempted to run after her like a child and ask her. But I'm a grown woman sadly, so I make the bed, head into the bathroom to brush my teeth and finally climb under the duvet.

Yet the moment I lie down, my fatigue evaporates. I don't feel like I'm going to catch a wink of sleep all night. A thought has planted itself in my brain and I can't get rid of it. That gun Robert found in the car after my accident – where did it come from? Was it my pistol? Did I have it with me back then? Eventually I drift off.

In the middle of the night, I get up, get dressed and leave Ira's apartment. The sky is clear and speckled with stars, the air crisp and cold. A thick layer of frost covers the parked vehicles like icing on a cake. The streetlights paint pale circles on the pavement. I get in my car and drive off, gliding noiselessly down empty roads and through the night.

It's easy enough to find the path from the car park to the water by the light of the stars.

Cold moonlight pours down on to the dark surface of the lake, which is as smooth as a mirror. The silence is so profound, I can practically hear my own heartbeat. To my right, I see the two tents.

Empty. And the bikes are gone. There's nobody here. My eyes scan my surroundings. Is that laughter I hear? No – it's just the wind blowing softly through the bare branches. I can feel it now too; it brushes over me, as gentle as a lover's caress. Goosebumps break out all over my body.

And then suddenly, as if from nowhere, they take shape before my eyes: Juli, Maike, Paul and Erik. Moving in silence, they form a circle around me like actors waiting onstage for the lights to go out and the curtain to lift. Spotlights shine, and the play can begin.

Maike steps forwards holding a gun, her face wet with tears. The first silent shot hits Paul; the second, Juli; and the third, Erik. I watch, paralysed with horror as blood soaks black into the ground.

Now Maike sees me too; she steps over the corpses and walks towards me.

'I waited for you,' she says. 'Three days and three nights I waited, praying every second that you'd come back for me.'

'I . . . I . . .' is all I can stutter.

'You promised.'

She raises the gun, takes aim at me. I sink to my knees and bury my face in my hands. 'I'm sorry,' I whisper. 'Forgive me.'

'You're going to die. Just like Paul and the others.'

I feel the hard barrel of the gun pressing into the back of my head.

'No, please don't!' I scream.

And then I bolt upright, drenched in sweat.

Where am I? My heart is pounding almost out of my chest. Fleeting phantasms drift through my mind, grow blurry and finally dissolve. Gradually it dawns on me that I've been having a nightmare. I lower my head back on to the pillow with a sigh of relief.

Some disturbing dream, that was.

Suddenly I'm wide awake. I leap out of bed. Where's that note I found in Alexander's house? I reach for my trousers, but pause in confusion when I realise they aren't my own. Of course – I got changed at my mother's place, so that's where the note with all those incomprehensible acronyms must be. I sit down on the edge of the bed. There was an M, I remember. M for Maike? Then it comes to me that the first letter was an I, followed by an M. IMTK, that was it. Plus a question mark. And suddenly I know what the letters stand for: is Maike the killer?

Was it actually Maike who murdered her friends? But why? Question after question bubbles up in my mind. I try to recall the scene from my nightmare, but I can't quite bring it into view.

Concentrate! What happened back then?

My mouth goes dry with anticipation. I'm on the brink of remembering the truth – I can feel it. Sleep is out of the question now. Cautiously I open the bedroom door and creep barefoot into the kitchen, where I take a bottle of water from the fridge before padding back to the guest room.

I take a large swig and shut my eyes. My head is whirring.

Suddenly a thought flashes to the front of my mind. I want to push it away for ever, but it forces its way through.

There could be a different explanation: the M on Alexander's note could also stand for Michaela.

33

'No,' I whisper. 'No, it's not possible.'

I've never had a gun other than my father's, and I still have that now. It proves beyond all doubt that it couldn't have been me. I repeat that to myself like a mantra, but my unease refuses to lift.

I leave Ira's guest room once again to creep into the living room and return carrying her phone. It's five in the morning; they're probably still asleep but I can't wait any longer. I need to know now. I dial the number and my mother picks up on the second ring.

'It's me, Mum. Michaela.'

'Oh, thank God. Where are you? I've been so worried. Please, just come home. We'll talk again, OK?'

'I need to speak to Robert. It's urgent,' I say, ignoring her words.

'He's asleep,' she answers, with obvious confusion.

'Then wake him up. It's really important.'

'Fine,' she says, drawing the word out. 'Hold on a second.'

I feel faint with anxiety, hoping beyond hope that Robert will give me the information I so desperately want. It feels like forever until I hear his voice.

'Hello, Michaela. You wanted to speak to me?' He sounds drowsy.

'What did you do with the gun you found in the car after the accident?'

'I—' He breaks into a coughing fit as he always does when he's worked up. Not a good sign.

'Well?' I urge him impatiently.

'I spent a long time debating what I should do with it,' he eventually recovers himself enough to say.

'Yes, and? What *did* you do?' Robert's typically awkward way of going round the houses to get to the point is making me jittery.

'At first I just wanted to throw it away, but then I thought it might be safest to put it back in its usual place.'

I swallow. 'Its usual place?'

'Yes – in the wooden box where you keep all the other mementoes of your father.'

'How do you know about that?'

'Your mother told me.'

I feel queasy.

'And you put the gun you found in the car back in my box?' I ask.

'Yes,' Robert wheezes. 'Your mother and I thought that if you missed it, you might ask where it got to and—'

I hang up. I'm standing stock-still in the middle of the room, my shoulders slumped. The phone slips out of my hand and thumps to the floor. I barely notice I'm doing it, but bend down anyway to pick it up.

No, my rational mind screams. *It's impossible. I am not a murderer! There must be another explanation.*

I get dressed in a trance-like state. Then I take the phone back to the living room and scribble a note for Ira on the pad next to the charging dock on the sideboard:

Dear Ira, thank you for everything. None of this is your fault.

Back in the hall, I slip on my boots, retrieve my coat and gun from the closet and quietly pull the apartment door closed behind me.

34

It's six-thirty by the time I steer the car off the motorway. Streams of commuters are already making their way towards Berlin, but my side of the road is fairly empty. I make quick progress. The car park comes into view in the twilight before dawn. I feel oddly emotionless, as if a switch has been flicked inside me. My head feels like it's full of cotton wool; not a single thought can gain purchase inside it.

Just a few yards down the narrow path, the icy dawn air starts to burn against my skin. My right hand grips my gun like a vice. Step by step, I drawer nearer to the lake. The memories rise of their own accord. My mind submerges into the past. It's summer – the summer of 2003.

Birds twitter in the forest. Dust tickles my nose and the scent of pine resin lingers in the air. The heat envelops me like the walls of an invisible prison.

I notice sounds: the cracking of branches, the creaking of the trees. I feel no fear. I continue down the path without hesitation.

In my hand, my fingers curl around my father's gun. I've brought it with me. I'm going to threaten to kill myself in front of Paul, prove to him how much I love him. Maybe then he'll finally realise that he loves me too. Wait – I can hear Paul's sarcastic laughter – or maybe it's more jeering than sarcastic. Is he mocking someone, telling the others about me? Are they all laughing at me? The idea stabs at my heart like a knife.

The path curves, grows wider; the forest begins to clear. Before me lies the lake, thin wraiths of mist rising from the surface. I walk on slowly.

To my right, the tents. Laughter. Seemingly endless laughter. The dog growls, runs at me with bared teeth. Do I pull the trigger? Yes, I do. It whines pitifully, legs buckling beneath its body. Juli bursts out of the tent and runs towards me, fists clenched.

I fire again.

At Juli.

At Paul.

At Erik.

No. I shake my head. This can't be what happened. There *was* a dog – he was called Corky – but I didn't see him. So how *did* it go? I rewind a little further through my memory.

I see Paul. He comes out of the tent, spots me, and his face turns to stone. He tells me to get lost, to leave him alone once and for all. Tells me I'm sick in the head. His mouth works angrily; a never-ending stream of venom pours out. I want him to stop, I scream at him to stop, but he keeps on and on and on. And then I pull the trigger. Now he's quiet. Juli and Erik stand as if paralysed, staring at me like I'm some kind of monster. Then they start screaming too. I fire again and again until everything's quiet.

The light of the breaking day turns the surface of the lake to silver. The fog is thick, takes a long time to clear. I feel warm now; it's going to be another sweltering day. I unzip my coat.

A bloodcurdling scream. Maike. Horror in her eyes. She's running away.

I stand on the shore of the lake and let my eyes wander over it. The rays of the rising sun make the water glitter – you'd think it was covered all over with thousands upon thousands of diamonds. A gentle breeze ruffles its surface. How beautiful it is, I think, and so very peaceful. I wade cautiously into the lake. The gun in my hand feels heavier and heavier.

Did I run after Maike? Yes, I did. She was quick, but I was quicker. She fought, but I was stronger. And I had my gun. I tied her to the tree. She had to die slowly and in agony to punish her for taking Paul away from me.

I left her to die in the forest.

The gun slips from my hand, hits the water with a splash. I watch it sink rapidly to the bottom. Then I move forwards, as if in slow motion. I part the surface with my hands and follow the little ripples out into the lake. Paul rises from the water beside me. He smiles and leads me by the hand. Now the others are here too: Juli, Erik and Maike. Their bodies float weightlessly around me, guiding me out into the depths of the lake.

The water closes over me. My feet lose contact with the floor. I feel heavy. So heavy. Paul holds me tight, embraces me, pulls me down with him into the dark, dark abyss. I breathe the water, drift with the current, sink deeper and deeper. Down into the void.

SIX MONTHS LATER

SIX-MONTHS LATER

Excerpt from an article in the
Berliner Tagesspiegel

Police Breakthrough in Cold Cases

Last night, detectives arrested two men on suspicion of having murdered a married couple sixteen years ago, along with their son (8) and daughter (15). Investigators believe the two suspects are guilty of further crimes, including the unsolved murder of four teenagers by a lake in Brandenburg near Berlin in 2003. In both cases, the killers bound and gagged a female victim and left her to die of exposure. At the time of the murders, the suspects were only fourteen and therefore below the age of criminal responsibility. As such, they cannot be held accountable under German law for either crime.

ACKNOWLEDGMENTS

First of all, I would like to thank my readers. I hope this book provided you with a few thrills and spills and that you're looking forward to more of my stories.

I'd also like to thank my test readers Anja Schubert, Anica Neumann, Simone Fischer, Bettina Reitz, Bettina Maraun, Juliette Manuela Braatz, Annette Lunau, Daniela Krüger, Tanja Schölzel and Claudia Gneissinger for helping me with such enthusiasm. You're the best – and I hope you'll be on board with my next thriller too.

Huge thanks in particular to my husband, Thomas Nommensen, who writes thrillers himself and once again stood by my side, both as my muse and as my first reader. I feel like our teamwork paid off, and thank goodness our marriage survived the process!

If you, dear reader, likewise feel that we've produced the kind of twists and suspense you want from a story, please leave a review on Amazon or send a few stars my way. For the latest news on my other titles, past and future, sign up for my newsletter on my website: jutta-maria-herrmann.de. And if you have any questions relating to this book, just drop me a line at jutta@jutta-maria-herrmann.de. I do my best to answer every email. I'm also on Facebook and Instagram, and it goes without saying that you can get in touch with me there too.

Facebook: https://www.facebook.com/ JuttaMariaHerrmannAutorin/
Instagram: https://www.instagram.com/jutta.maria.herrmann/
I'd love to hear from you!
Jutta Maria Herrmann

ABOUT THE AUTHOR

Born in the Saarland, Germany, Jutta Maria Herrmann is a trained bookseller and has a degree in German language and literature. During her career she has organised rock concerts, scrubbed floors, been a secretary for a joinery firm, worked at a conservation centre in Berlin, written scripts for dubbed films, and much more besides. Nowadays she earns a crust as an assistant to the politics section of a newspaper, but whenever she has time, she sits down at her computer and writes stories.

For more information, visit www.jutta-maria-herrmann.de.

In 2019 her thriller *The Evil In You* won the Kindle Storyteller Award in Germany.

ABOUT THE TRANSLATOR

Jozef van der Voort is a literary translator working from Dutch and German into English. He is an alumnus of the New Books in German Emerging Translators Programme, was named runner-up in the Harvill Secker Young Translators' Prize in 2014, and won second prize in the 2020 Geisteswissenschaften International Non-Fiction Translation competition.